For my wife Rachel,

Our three princes,

And our little princess.

Love to all.

The Circus Ax, A Novel

By

Timothy A. Westrick

CHAPTER ONE

Thursday, June 8, 1922

The buzzing of the mosquitos seemed to be
competing with the chirping of the crickets in the early
evening, a cacophony which could grow deafening when
the brood of seventeen-year cicadas jealously participated.
Once the whistle faded from the 6:58 Michigan United
Railway train on the Jackson-to-Battle Creek line, the
insects took over. It had so far been a hot and wet late
Spring, keeping down the dust from the predominantly
unpaved side streets through town, but encouraging the

generation of these small annoyances. Sitting on one's open front porch with a lit oil lamp was done at one's own risk, as the light attracted nearly every type of indigenous bug.

Some people in town were better at handling the nuisance. The woman walking down Winthrop Street, seemingly oblivious to the pests, was Ms. Alice Mallett. Not much disturbed Ms. Mallett, not the weather, nor her demanding work, and certainly not God's tiniest creations. She had a confident gait and offered a friendly tip of her chin under her straw hat to those she passed on the sidewalk, most of whom knew her by name.

Jackson was a fair size city, the third largest in the state, with a population of around 73,000. Although considerably smaller than Detroit, the numerous railroads which crossed through Jackson kept it metropolitan, by this state's standards. Business and development had been aided by the railroads as well as the plentiful labor provided by the influx of Welsh, Irish, German, and Polish immigrants. Additionally, the state penal system provided many hands doing hard labor at the Southern Michigan Prison at Jackson for usually no more than forty cents a day, hired out to businesses and companies building the "skyscrapers" downtown. With prison reform, that source of workers dried up, but the continual tide of immigrants pushing West filled the need sufficiently.

If Michigan were a person's right hand, as most Jackson would be somewhere in the palm, nearer the wrist than the knuckles. The use of the hand was something learned by most Michiganders as children, an easy way to describe the geography to those not familiar with the state.

The community was made up mostly of long-term families, and one's family history meant something in this society. Stately homes in town, and farms in the rolling hills surrounding the city, were known by family name, as opposed to addresses and lot numbers. It seemed as though the same names had been running the businesses and politics of the city for years, only the Roman numerals behind the names changing with the generations.

As the centennial anniversary of the founding of the area by a New Yorker, Horace Blackman, in July of 1829 was approaching, there had been much talk of those earlier days. Most had roots going back to that founding of Jacksonburg, which later became Jacksonopolis, and finally shortened in 1838 to simply Jackson. While being named for Democratic president Andrew Jackson, the city boasted being the birthplace of the Republican Party in 1854, pinpointed as occurring at the corner of Franklin Street and Second.

Regardless of the fact that the centennial was still a few years off, the community chose to make it a multi-year celebration. The tri-colored bunting on the Greenwood Avenue Methodist Episcopal Church and in front of City Hall would fade, tear, and be replaced more than once before the actual anniversary of the founding.

Despite the air about her, Ms. Mallett's picture would not be found in any past issues of "The Reflector," the Jackson High School yearbook, nor was there a home referred to as The Mallett Home, as she was a relative newcomer to the area.

The thirty-five year old had arrived in Michigan from Oregon six years previously, coming East to work at the YWCA first in Flint, and then Bay City. Working as matron at the Florence Crittendon Home on Lansing Avenue is what finally brought her to Jackson, where she also conducted Sunday school classes. The home was associated with the relatively new Child Welfare League of America, and provided for service to homeless and needy children, single women, and "delinquent" girls. Some

considered her to be a bluenose, a real prude. Others didn't

think her abstinence from spirits a sin nor crime,

considering the Eighteenth Amendment was the law of the

land, and many Michigan counties had been dry for years.

Alice Mallett walked casually down Winthrop, her

parasol closed and held by her side, tapping the sidewalk

with every other step. She wore a light dress and a coat

despite the heat. As she came to the front walk at 511

Winthrop, she turned towards the steps, walked up, and

rapped on the screen door. These days, main doors were

rarely closed during the warm months, and virtually never

locked. Most homes didn't even have deadbolts or other

locks.

"Oh, hello, Alice," Adelle Welch said, welcoming

her friend into her house. Welch held the door and stepped

back as Mallett squeezed past, heading through the entry to

the parlor.

"So nice of you to have me over for a glass of lemonade," Mallett said, setting her parasol down into a brass umbrella stand beside the couch. As she took a seat, Mrs. Welch picked up a glass pitcher set on a lace doily in the center of the low coffee table. The hardwood beneath the table was covered by a busy American Sarouk Persian carpet which had been a surprise wedding anniversary gift from Mrs. Welch's parents. She filled two glasses, concentrating on not splashing the fresh-squeezed drink when chunks of ice passed over the lip of the pitcher.

"Can you believe those mosquitos, Adelle?" Ms. Mallett asked. "I thought we grew them big out West, but the pesky ones around here are truly dreadful." While personally, Mallett ignored them, the insects were the chief topic of discussion these days.

"You get used to them, Alice," Mrs. Welch

commented. "My father would tell us stories about when he was working as an engineer on the Panama Canal. The mosquitoes down there could darn near carry a hen off, with some of her eggs for good measure."

"Truly, Adelle, men tell the tallest of tales," Ms. Mallett said between sips from her glass. "How has your day been?"

"Stitching dresses, even with my new Singer, has got my fingers aching," Mrs. Welch lamented, referring to her occupation as a seamstress. "But the business is busy, and that's the bee's knees to me. No matter how much money you make, there's always more than enough ways to spend it."

The Welchs had two sons currently attending the Jackson Business University, and the finer things did not escape Mrs. Welch's attention. The frugal Ms. Mallett was too polite to point this out, nor the fact that she got along just fine with her humble stipend.

"And how was your day, Alice?"

"Just fine," Ms. Mallett responded. "I worked on menus for the next week, and was downtown making arrangements for the annual Crittendon dinner." The dinner was as much a social event as it was a fund-raiser for the Home, and its popularity justified a great deal of Mallett's May and June work being devoted to the function. "All this running around, my dogs are tired."

"Don't allow that Ada Smith to work you too hard, Alice," Mrs. Welch advised, referring to the Crittendon Home's superintendent.

"Not to worry, Adelle," the always amiable woman said. She was not one to complain too much. Although not unattractive, Ms. Mallett was unwed with few suitors calling, so work was her passion. Her young looks and lack of a husband actually seemed to help her in her dealings with the temporary residents as they passed through Crittendon.

Mrs. Welch and Ms. Mallett gossiped as they sipped their lemonades, the sun gently falling beneath the elms down the block on Edward Street. They discussed the summer dresses at Cook & Feldher Apparel, the sale on "College Girl" corsets at the Jackson Corset Company factory salesroom on West Cortland Street, and the new women's footwear at Jacobson's. There was an upcoming art exhibition in Ann Arbor they both wanted to see, and a gallon of milk was up to a half-dollar at Ellsworth's Pharmacy. These were the topics of discussion for which front parlors were designed, not to speak ad nauseam about insects.

A baseball game was airing on the Aeriola Senior in another room of the house, loud enough to be heard outside in the yard. After individual trips to the first floor powder room, and the announcement that the Detroit Tigers had defeated the Philadelphia Athletics seven to six, the ladies developed a taste for something cold and sweet, a taste not sated by the tart lemonade.

"Let's go get some ice cream," Mrs. Welch suggested. "Henry's got his hammering to do, and I haven't been out of the house all day."

Mr. Welch was taking advantage of the longer late Spring days to construct a garage. As automobile ownership expanded across the country, so too did the need for shelter for people's investments on wheels. Mr. Welch's pride and joy was a recently-acquired Buick Model 10, assembled by the Whiting Motor Car Company at the former Buick plant right there in Jackson. To Adelle Welch's occasional dismay, Mr. Welch doted on the 4-cylinder machine like it was one of their children. But she was an advocate of compromise, and as Mr. Welch indulged Adelle her Sunday teas and late-evening walks to the ice cream shop, she chose to give him ample leave for his "hobbies." At least he wasn't out downing Canadian whiskey and chasing young flappers in their Betty Wales dresses.

"Wonderful idea, Adelle," Ms. Mallett responded. "I need to pick up a couple dozen eggs before heading back to Crittendon tonight, anyway."

"Just let me get my cheaters," Mrs. Welch said, collecting her glasses from a side table.

It was a short walk to Davison's Drug Store on Granson Street near Steward Avenue. Between Davison's and The Sugar Bowl, there were plenty of people out for cold refreshment. The line wasn't too long in Davison's, but it was well past sunset by the time they finished their ice cream, each daintily spooning melting vanilla from pewter bowls.

Before leaving the store, Ms. Mallett bought two dozen eggs and a small bunch of dwarf lake irises, the transaction costing her just over a dollar. She requested an itemized receipt from the clerk behind the counter so she could seek reimbursement for the eggs she was purchasing for the Home. More importantly, she did not want the demanding Mrs. Ada Smith to think that Alice was attempting to get her flower's on Crittendon's nickel. She carried her purchases and purse in a sack in one hand, her parasol in the other.

"Shall I escort you back to the Home?" Mrs. Welch asked her companion as the two women took in the bright moonlight. Although neither carried a timepiece, they agreed that it was some time after ten o'clock.

"Thank you, no," Ms. Mallett told her friend. "It'll be out of your way, and it's bright enough yet. Besides, you should make sure that husband of yours hasn't smashed any fingers with his hammer."

"For the sake of the neighbors," Mrs. Welch said, "I just hope he's put his tools up for the night. Lord knows he's kept me up with that ruckus before, taking care of the 'jalopy,' as he lovingly calls it. By the way, Alice, that Robinson Circus has their last day in town tomorrow. They pull stakes and head for Ohio Saturday morning, I believe. Won't you join Henry and me?"

"I've got plans with Mary Hagdon," Mallett explained. "I ran into Mary downtown this afternoon and we made plans to dine at The Central Café. But maybe after I'll meet you there."

"Okay, my dear, we'll hopefully see you there," Mrs. Welch said, waving a gloved hand.

"Take care, Adelle," Ms. Alice Mallett said, as she spoke with her friend for the last time. Ms. Mallett would not be seeing Mary Hagdon for pot roast at The Central

Café, nor Adelle and her husband at the circus the following day. In fact, Ms. Mallett did not see another soul on her walk home that night until she made the acquaintance of a stranger with malice on his brain under the milky blue light of the moon.

*****

About the time Alice Mallett was headed home with her eggs and flowers, Robert J. Brockie was pulling his automobile into his driveway at 1211 Lansing Avenue. He walked to the front door with his wife, enjoying the cooler evening despite the bugs. His three children scrambled up the front steps, hands and faces sticky from cotton candy, dutifully rushing upstairs since it was well past their bedtime.

The John Robinson Circus had been in town for a couple days, and Mr. and Mrs. Brockie had promised to take their children before it left Jackson for its next engagement. So that was how they had spent their evening

after Mr. Brockie got home from his job at Crandall

Electric on West Main. It was a fine way to start off the

children's summer break from school, before they went off

to Brockie's parent's farm in Ypsilanti. Summer at the

homestead of the grandparents meant weeks of milking

diary cows, swimming in one of the many small lakes

dotting the countryside, and watching the newsreels at the

single screen theater. While the children were there, Robert

Brockie and his wife Elizabeth would climb into their 1919

Buick Coupe and head to the country to visit on the

weekends, both of them genuinely envious of the carefree

summer weeks their children enjoyed.

Robert Brockie handed his wife a box of Cracker

Jack, a picture of Sailor Jack and Bingo his dog on the front

panel of the box.

"Put these up high in the pantry, Elizabeth," Brockie

instructed his wife. "The boys will just fight over the prize."

"And for Heaven's sake," Elizabeth Brockie said, taking the box, "those boys have had plenty of sweets tonight. If it weren't for the energy they burned riding the ponies at the circus, they'd be bouncing off the walls with all that sugar in their stomachs."

"Ah, the little fellas need to have some fun."

"They'll have fun all summer with your mother and father spoiling them rotten."

"Come now, Elizabeth," Mr. Brockie soothed his wife, taking her arm. "Count your blessings, because there's bound to be someone out there having a worse evening."

Robert and Elizabeth Brockie climbed the stairs to the second floor, checked on their boys, and retired to their own room at the back of the house. Shortly thereafter, the entire household was fast asleep, oblivious to anything occurring beyond the walls of their home.

*****

Detectives Juan Piper and Sean Timmons of the City of Jackson Police Department stood smoking Camel cigarettes from a pack Piper had in his coat pocket, that coat now draped over his left arm, enjoying being a little cooler in his shirtsleeves.

Both men looked the part of the authority, standing over six feet tall, matching fresh crew cuts from Howard's Barber Shop, although Piper's hair ran darker. They stood on an otherwise unremarkable street corner, smoking and talking, nothing other than their presence necessarily giving any indication to it having been the scene of an assault.

"It's good, but I'm not walking no mile for one," Timmons said, referencing the brand's popular slogan while examining the cigarette.

"I'm usually a Lucky Strike man," Piper responded, "but it's all they had at Davison's." Piper knew that his fellow detective wasn't picky about what he smoked as long as it had been bummed from someone else and hadn't cost him a penny.

"Hey, boys," Officer Clifford Hockman called out from a black patrol wagon. When the vehicle had been delivered many years ago from the Jackson Auto Company, Hockman had been designated as the driver, and had been employed primarily in that capacity ever since. While the Jackson Police Department now had a veritable fleet of wagons and patrol cars, not to mention a stable of horses for the mounted patrol still serviced by the J.E. Woodruff's City Shoeing Shop, Hockman was always referred to as the first driver. He wasn't much of a policeman, but his years behind the wheel had made him rather proficient in negotiating the sometimes treacherous roads in the motorized wagon.

"Sure, Cliff," Timmons said, "take her on home."

"Thank you, sir," a quiet and timid voice called out from the back of the wagon. The detectives waved and the 1911 vehicle chugged away down South Elm Avenue. The voice belonged to Ms. Martha Quick, a young lady of twenty-one years who had been accosted a short time prior to the arrival of the police. She had a short bob haircut and a short skirt with a low waistline, trends which were creeping into the Midwest from New York and Chicago. In fact, Ms. Quick had acquired both from the Illinois big city.

Piper and Timmons had been enjoying a quiet night at the station, one reading *The Citizen Patriot*, the other scanning that morning's *The Jackson News*. When done with the local papers, both of them would pick up a word-cross page from a stack of old New York *World* Sunday newspapers. The puzzles were solved sparingly, and in pencil so that answers could be erased and the other detective could work on it. But for Forrest Badgley, a local attorney who worked out of the National Union Bank Building, bringing a few copies back from trips to New York City, the availability of *World* newspapers was quite limited.

Being in the basement of the County Building on West Michigan Avenue, the police station remained relatively cool during the hot late Spring and Summer days and evenings.

The disadvantage to being below the ground was that the three cells of the holding area tended to flood when the snow melted in March, or with the heavy rains in April and May. Piper had, with his own money, purchased a Polar Cub desk fan which helped keep the musty air circulating. The detective frequently reminded Chief Bean of his personal sacrifice for the common good, going above and beyond to acquire the fan without tapping the city budget. Timmons didn't think much of his partner's good nature. The fan was made by the A.C. Gilbert Company, so it came with a free Erector Set which Piper wanted for his son.

The call had come in shortly before ten o'clock that night, an assault complaint, which roused the detectives to the street. Normally, the uniformed patrol officer walking the beat with his bowler hat and billy club would have taken the victim's statement and dropped the complaint off at the end of his shift. However, this wasn't the first such complaint of the week in the usually quiet and peaceful Michigan city.

"What's that, number four?" Timmons asked his partner as the wagon turned the corner off of Elm and disappeared from view, although the back-firing of the engine was still audible.

"Three, counting the one Monday in the Drexel addition," Piper responded, stubbing his cigarette out on the walk. "Third time this week some fella's been sweet enough on a woman walking down the street to try and jump her."

"Well, that last one was a real Sheba. I can understand him going for her."

"Sean, if you hadn't been reading the paper across the room from me, I would be asking where you were around nine-thirty tonight."

"I said she was spiffy," Timmons explained. "I think a lot of dames are spiffy. Don't mean I go nuts at the sight of a nice pair of gams and try to drag the lady off."

"I tell you what'll happen if we have another," Piper mused, looking up at the moon, bright enough to make him squint as his pupils narrowed.

"Tell me, you been playing with the Ouija board?

Seeing the future?" Timmons chided. "Pastor Parrott at St. Paul's says that a-cult stuff's trouble. Reverend Griffith ain't too fond of it, neither."

"The Occult, Sean," Piper corrected him. "One more keen lady's going to get her petticoat ruffled by this guy. Then Crary's going to get the complaint, and he'll pester Hatch," he said, referring to the City Manager and the Prosecuting Attorney, respectfully. "He'll put the pressure on Chief Bean for us to pinch somebody for this, and if not, he'll call up Colonel Vandercook and call in the calvary."

"So the State Police boys work on this one, big deal," Timmons commented, dismissing his partner's concerns. "Don't we have some real bad fellas to track down, get shipped off to the Michigan State pen down the road. Be a shame not to fill it up behind those high walls. This groping maniac wouldn't get sent to the largest walled maximum security facility in the country. He'll do thirty days in the county lock-up and be on his way. Maybe ship him off to the looney bin in Ionia, at best. You want to waste time tracking a guy who probably wants to get free room and board from the county for a month?"

"I'm not saying he's a Sacco and Vanzetti, Sean," Detective Piper said. "But this guy is going to turn into a problem if we don't pinch him soon."

"The next Roscoe Arbuckle? Fine, Juan, let's get in the Flivver and head back to the office, figure out what we want to do about this guy."

The two detectives walked to the nearest driveway in which was parked one of the Department's newer Fords. It was a 1921 Touring T. The Chief's brother owned a dealership in East Lansing, and that had to have been the only reason for this particular purchase. There was no driver's side door, so both men had to step up on the running board on the right and climb in, Timmons, the driver, getting in first. The detectives imagined that this inconvenience prevented the dealer from selling it, so he unloaded it on his brother. At least the Chief had sprung for the electric starter, saving many a broken thumb or arm on a starting crank.

The procedure of starting it without the crank, however, was still tiresome and complicated, which sometimes encouraged the detectives to envy the mounted patrol and their horses. Raised on a horse farm not far from Kalamazoo, Piper would have joined the mounted patrol, except it paid a few nickels less than his detective position. Timmons opened the fuel line and then commenced to fiddle with the choke, key, throttle and spark lever all before pressing the starter button.

While the front of the automobile was cramped, at least the view from the bench, which rested atop the ten

gallon fuel tank, was high and unobstructed. Even in the
dim light from the street lamps, Timmons was able to deftly
avoid the hazards in the street. Besides pits caused by
missing cobblestones, other obstacles left in the roadway
included reminders that many of the merchants in town still
utilized horse-drawn wagons to transport their wares.

Piper lit another cigarette and appeared to Timmons
to still be brooding on the prospect of their unknown
assailant continuing to terrorize Jackson's female populace.

"Come on, Juan," Timmons said, taking his eyes off
the road. "It ain't like this guy's gonna kill one of these
dames."

"Horseshit, Sean," Piper said.

"What? You think he will?"

"No, Sean, you just ran through some."

CHAPTER TWO

Friday, June 9, 1922

Full sunrise was still half an hour away, but Robert Brockie was up to collect the milk delivery, before even the screeching rooster in the neighbor's backyard coop was up. There was many a morning when he'd awake to that miserable sound, the bird strutting around the neighbor's well-tended garden, pacing along the fence behind his house on the corner of Lansing Avenue and Jefferson Street. If it wouldn't turn out to be tough meat, Brockie often told his wife that he'd show up after work with a chicken with a freshly-wrung neck for the stew pot.

This morning, as dawn was breaking behind his house to the east, the rooster was neither making a ruckus, nor stomping around the garden. Out of habit, he looked around for his usual early morning companion, who often found his way into Brockie's own garden to wreck havoc. This morning, however, Brockie did not see the rooster, only parallel rows in the soft soil amid the petunias and clay flowerpots, as if the blades of a small plow had been dragged through. Footprints accompanied the drag marks and further aroused Brockie's curiosity. He hadn't been walking through the garden, and his boys knew better than to trample in the manure-fertilized dirt.

Bent at the waist and straining to see in the dim light, he could barely make out an object set against one of the pots. No stranger to working the fields and the woods, it didn't take long for Brockie to make it out as a long-handled ax, a tool he did not own. The head was partially sunk into the tilled earth with the handle propped against the flowerpot. As his eyes adjusted to the light, the blood on the ax, the plants, and soaked into the ground around it became evident. For a moment he wondered if another vigilante neighbor had had enough of the rooster.

Brockie followed the furrows in the ground which ended at the grass of the front lawn, but the trail continued in matted blood, and then onto the sidewalk. Then he stepped onto the walk, careful to avoid stepping in the mess. No chicken, he knew from slaughtering them on the farm where he grew up, could have bled this much.

Several feet away, under the big oak at the edge of his yard, Brockie could make out what appeared to be a man's body. It was unusual, but not terribly alarming. Not knowing what to expect, Brockie decided to seek assistance from his neighbor Chester Horton, the owner of the annoying feathered creature. Regardless that these were days of temperance and prohibition, it was unfortunately not uncommon to come across a drunk who had imbibed to excess at a local speakeasy or country still. They were not always the most agreeable when awoken, so an extra pair of

hands to toss him into the street and get him on his way
would come in hand. Brockie did not care to have his wife
and boys see this type of riff-raff in their own yard.
Besides, the queer business in the garden had Brockie on
edge.

"Chester," Robert Brockie called, rapping on his
neighbor's side screen door. "Chester, it's Bob Brockie."
He tried to speak audibly, but not be disrespectful of the
early morning quiet.

"How do, Bob," Horton said, coming to the door.
"Bit early to be going door to door selling Fuller brushes,
ain't it?" he quipped. He was dressed only in an undershirt
and shorts. Horton was a widower in his seventies, as best
as Brockie could tell of his neighbor's age. Brockie knew
that his neighbor had served in the 13th Michigan Infantry
during the Civil War, and still carried around a
secessionist's *Minie* ball in his hip. He was, however, as

tough an old man as his rooster would be to eat. Despite

his age and advanced belly spilling over the waistband of

his skivvies, more than fifty years working the rails made

him as hard as the spikes he used to drive into the railroad

ties when laying track.

"You caught me in my drawers having my oatmeal.

What's giving you the heebie-jeebies, Bob?"

"I think I got some fella passed out under my oak

tree, Chester. Figured I could use some help rousting him,

if you aren't too occupied."

"What do you mean you 'think', Bob?"

"I haven't checked him out yet, Chester," Brockie

said. "Looks like the fella might have taken a spill and hurt

himself."

"Sure thing, Bob," Horton said. "Hell, it's

becoming a weekly ritual. I think somebody's running a

gin mill out of their basement around here. Maybe Clyde

Murphy down on Clinton Road, from the looks of that rosy

nose of his. That, and the sumbitch is always in such a

good mood." Horton opened the screen door and stepped

out in his bare feet.

"Don't you think you ought to grab your trousers,

Chester?" Brockie inquired.

"Christ Almighty, Bob, I don't think I'll offend the

sensibilities of some drunkard out cold on your lawn. Only

folks out this early are working men and insomniacs, and if

they want to check out an old man in his shorts, then they

take the risk."

"You didn't happen to misplace an ax, did you,

Chester?" Brockie asked.

"A what? I look like Paul Bunyan to you?"

"Never mind," Brockie said, used to Horton's dry

wit.

The two men walked down Horton's short drive to

the front walk and moved towards the corner, coming upon the body. They both paused as what was before them became clear, the amorphous shape of lumps and folds of clothing giving way to the curves of a woman's body and surrounding gore. It was now evident that there was no movement from breathing.

"Good Lord," Chester Horton said, shocked at the sight, rocking back on his bare heels. He crossed himself, despite not having been in a house of worship for at least twenty years.

"Easy, Chester," Brockie said. While certainly disturbed by the scene, Brockie seemed calm and business like. He had seen horrors of the Great War while with the American Expeditionary Force led by "Black Jack" Pershing. The Meuse-Argonne Offensive had left Brockie partially numb to trauma and death. But seeing a Doughboy torn to pieces by one of Hiram Maxim's

Maschinengewehr was still different than finding a mostly naked woman in a pool of blood in the front yard.

"Where's her face, Bob?"

"Never you mind about that, Chester," Brockie responded. "Just go on down to Clyde's and get the police out here." While Clyde Murphy might have been running a gin mill out of his basement, he was still a value to the neighborhood since he had an Automatic Electric Type 21 candlestick telephone in his parlor.

"Okay, Bob," Chester responded unsteadily, moving down the sidewalk in his undershorts with his head turned, unable to pull his eyes away from the body.

Brockie looked around the area as the sky began to lighten. While there was no street light nearby, details began to reveal themselves with the rising sun. Exposed skin seemed to glow in the faint light, dark in spots where covered in what Brockie presumed to be blood. The dead woman's clothing had been forcefully torn open, and a light coat sat in a rumpled pile closer to the street.

On the other side of the garden, beneath the low branches of an oak, he saw a shopping sack, something wet oozing through the canvas material, and a parasol in the grass. These were items he had not seen when first investigating the footprints and ax in the garden. Nearby there also appeared to be a purse, it's contents strewn about as if having been dumped in a wild search for valuables.

Having seen enough for the time being, Robert Brockie went back into his house to retrieve the box of Crack Jack from the pantry. He sat on the front steps, waiting for the authorities to arrive, absently feeling through the caramel-coated popcorn and peanuts for a more benign surprise than the one he had just discovered. Brockie jumped to his feet with a start, spilling the box, toy surprise and all, when Horton's rooster squawked from its fence post.

*****

By seven-thirty, the corner of Lansing Avenue and
Jefferson Street was crowded with personnel from various
agencies. Uniformed patrol officers from the city police
department were the first on the scene, being directed to the
location by Chester Horton and Clyde Murphy. Chester
was a bit more steady when he got back, strengthened
mostly by the charitable donation of a couple shots of rye
from Clyde's private barrel of hooch.

Deputies from the Jackson County Sheriff's
Department, directed by Undersheriff Vern Kutt, arrived at
the same time as Detective Timmons, narrowly avoiding a
collision at the nearby intersection. As the entire country
was relatively new to motorized travel, traffic accidents
were a common occurrence.

"Son of a bitch," Timmons said upon seeing the

body under the tree. A patrolman lifted a blood-soaked sheet which had been modestly draped over the dead woman. "Piper ain't gonna let me forget he was right."

Since the Sheriff's Department didn't have much in the way of a detective squad, and the location of Lansing and Jefferson was firmly nestled within the city limits of Jackson, there would be no jurisdictional squabble over the investigation, unless the Michigan Department of State Police decided to put their ante into the pot. In fact, the case would prove to be a splendid example of inter-departmental cooperation.

"Where's Piper?" Kutt asked the detective. Kutt must have eaten his Quaker Quakies growing up, as his stature dwarfed even Timmons. Kutt's sleeves of his khaki deputy uniform were rolled up over his beefy forearms, exposing bluing tattoos from his military days.

"On the way," Timmons answered. "Somebody go

to wake up Doc Mills, yet?"

"Yeah," Kutt said. "Blake went to pick up the coroner. A woman, huh? Bad news is gonna travel fast. At least the morning copy of the *News* is already out," he said, talking about the morning *Jackson News*, the only morning publication in the region at the time.

"Sure," Timmons agreed, "but the *Patriot* will have a special edition this afternoon if they get the scoop. 'Course, maybe they can help."

Timmons knelt beside the corpse to get a closer look, batting at the flies which had begun congregating. A woman's straw hat rested near the body, which he picked up to inspect the red-lined gash through the crown. A corresponding wound was present in the top of the woman's skull, the hair was matted and damp. A rough slash crossing her pale throat looked like a red velvet choker the whores wore out at the roadhouse on the outskirts of Jackson County. Not that Timmons had any first-hand knowledge, he'd be sure to tell anyone listening to his thoughts. Her dress and corset had been torn open, buttons which had popped from their stitches were sprinkled throughout the folds.

"Sean," a voice said from behind Timmons.

"Don't say it, Juan. I'll say it. Our guy's crossed over from grabbing a teet to bumping off dames. Just like Vern said, bad news."

"Mills on the way?"

"Yeah. Think we ought to call in Col. Vandercook's men?"

"Sure," Piper agreed. They already knew that they should get all the help they could. Hacked-up women on the city streets of Jackson would certainly raise the hue and cry for swift justice. He waved over the patrolman who had been holding up the bloody sheet.

"Round up Captain Fagan," Piper instructed the young officer. "Ask him to call in the State boys. Who's the top guy at the local post?" Piper asked Timmons.

"Art Treece," was the answer. "We ought to get a call into the State Police H.Q. in Lansing, too. Get the bloodhounds here by the afternoon, try and get a scent."

The detectives ordered the other uniformed officers to spread out in a line and search the property for anything of note. The suspected murder weapon, a long handled ax, had already been pointed out by Robert Brockie, and a deputy stood guard over it.

As other items were discovered, Piper or Timmons were called over to inspect them. Besides the probable weapon, they mainly wanted to find clues to the victim's identity. Posting a photograph of the savaged body at City Hall to see if any of the citizenry recognized her just wouldn't do here in Jackson. The affluent residents on the west side of Grand River were big on civility and decorum.

Timmons was called over to a wet sack on the sidewalk, opposite the garden. Squatting down beside it, he used a stick to lift open the sack. Having been bitten once by a possum after blindly sticking his hand into a dark crawlspace a few years ago, he always looked first. The partial numbness in his fingers always tingled to remind him of the incident.

"Couple dozen eggs, or so, cracked," he said, and began to poke through the slimy contents. "A handful of flowers. Got a receipt," he announced, drawing Piper over.

They both looked at the piece of paper Timmons held out in front of him, soggy with egg yolk but still legible. Handwritten in pencil was a list of purchases along with a tally down one side. Preprinted at the top was Davison's. Timmons handed the receipt to his partner and went over to the empty purse and it's contents littered around it.

The litter mostly consisted of miscellaneous papers. There were several sheets with the names of days neatly printed at the top margins, a list and description of meals below. They appeared to Timmons to be cafeteria menus, neatly written in script. One stiff piece of paper appeared to be an invitation for the annual Crittendon Home Dinner. Timmons took a closer look at an envelope and showed it to Piper.

"Addressed to Miss A. Mallett," he said, "care of the Florence Crittendon Home, 1603 Lansing Avenue. Return address is someplace in Oregon. Think she's one of them unwed mothers who live at the home?"

"No," Piper answered. "Her clothes, or at least what's left of them, are too nice. You got a bastard to take care of, the people at Crittendon aren't going to let you blow your dough on nice dresses. You know who is in charge down there?"

"Ada Smith," Timmons said. "She belongs to my church."

"Well," Piper said, once again fishing his cigarettes out of his pocket, ignoring Timmons with his outstretched hand, "she's the lucky lady this morning who gets to lose her appetite just before breakfast. You want to bring her down here for the identification?"

"Shouldn't we wait until Doc Mills and Seybold get a chance to clean her up a bit?"

"Gonna waste time doing that," Piper said. "Besides, if your Mrs. Smith runs a house full of bastards and round-heeled Shebas, she ought to be able to handle this."

CHAPTER THREE

Friday, June 9, 1922

Inspector Arthur Treece was in his mid-thirties, lean

and tall with his height emphasized by his Stetson atop his

head and the leather riding boots on his feet. A few

hundred miles west and a decade or two back, he'd fit

perfectly in the role of a fast-draw in a gold rush town. As

an investigating detective, Treece wore a brown wool suit,

instead of the blue uniform and cordovan leather Sam

Browne belt worn by other troopers.

He was the top man at the Michigan Department of

State Police post just outside the Jackson city limits, and

Treece was consequently responsible for both conducting

criminal investigations, as well as being in charge of the

supervision of the approximately thirty troopers who also

worked out of the post. It was a well-staffed contingent

considering that the total number of MDSP troopers under

Col. Roy C. Vandercook was less than 500 men throughout

the roughly ninety-eight thousand square miles of the state

of Michigan.

The Michigan Department of State Police had been

founded in 1917 by Governor Sleeper, known at that time

as the Michigan State Troops Permanent Force or

Constabulary. Despite its title, the force had originally

been formed as a temporary wartime domestic security

body. Two years after its founding, the MDSP became a

permanent law enforcement agency with state-wide

jurisdiction.

With the introduction of the automobile, the State

Police added a motorized unit to its mounted and

dismounted troops. Treece had served in the U.S. Army,

Calvary, during the War, and served out his enlistment at

Camp Custer in Battle Creek, before joining that city's

police force. Col. Vandercook had an affinity for former Calvary men, so Treece managed to join the MDSP from virtually its inception. He was assigned to the mounted unit until trading in his spurs for a Model T. He still sported the hat and boots of a rider, and the bulge on his hip beneath his suit coat was his trusty Colt from the War. A six-shooter, he admitted, would have been a better fit with his attire.

Art Treece drove into downtown Jackson, after finally getting the call to assist with a homicide. He'd been sitting in the woods waiting to nab a fugitive from justice. John "Little Bear" Smith was a Potawatomi Indian who had a taste for grain alcohol and threatening Circuit Court judges. Being six-six and over three hundred pounds, his Indian name was definitely a misnomer. Having spent time in the state prisons in Jackson and upstate in Marquette for violent offenses, Smith's threats were to be taken seriously.

Treece had gotten set up in an old tree stand used for hunting whitetail within view of Smith's ramshackle hut before sunrise, waiting for his fugitive to sleep off his usual binge of firewater. Just after eleven a four-door Dodge Brothers touring sedan came thundering down the road, Trooper Harold Mulbar honking his horn and waving his arm out the window. The vehicle grew larger, and louder, the closer it got, the MDSP emblem visible on the front driver's door when the dirt road jogged to the right for a short distance. The commotion negated the time and stealth Treece had expended this morning sitting on Little Bear's place. The inspector could hear the window at the rear of the shack break as the Indian made his escape into the woods, and with that his attempt this time was over. Smith knew the woods like a woman knows the crow's feet around her eyes. Trying to track him with anything short of a dozen troopers was just foolishness, the kind that got a hatchet buried in your back.

Inspector Treece parked in front of the Health Department administration building which was just up the block from the County Building where the police department was housed. Entering the brick and sandstone building, he was greeted by a collection of uniformed city officers, county deputies, and some troopers under his command. He briefly wondered what good such a display of law enforcement was if all they did was stand around whistling "Carolina in the Morning" with their hands in their pockets and cigarettes perched on their lips.

Trooper Mulbar waved, apparently a favorite motion of his, standing among three of his State Police collegues. At the break-neck speed and recklessness he operated the Department's Dodge, Treece wasn't surprised that his subordinate had beat him to the morgue in record time.

"Mulbar," Treece addressed his man.

"Yes, Inspector?"

"Say 'how'."

"How," Mulbar said with uncertainty, a curious look on his freshly-shaven face.

"Now you're qualified to track down Little Bear Smith. Since you spooked him off, I don't want to see your mug around the post until you bring him into it in shackles."

Mulbar's curious smile evaporated. Treece was fair and even-handed, but demanded a lot. Proud. Service. Excellence, Integrity and Courtesy. That would eventually become the department's motto, and Treece demanded such professionalism from his men.

The other troopers chuckled at their fellow officer's public dressing-down, although the laughter dried up quickly when Treece ordered the other three to assist

Mulbar in his duty of bringing in the fugitive. Fugitive warrant work was at time boring, but also potentially dangerous, especially when tracking a violent felon. The men were less than pleased.

Treece walked down a set of long, narrow steps which led to the morgue in the basement of the building. Between the morgue and the City police department, Treece spent most of his time in one downtown basement or another when working outside of his post. Down a dank hallway, Treece followed the murmur of voices and clanging of metal instruments in porcelain-coated trays and bowls. It could have been a cafeteria on the other side of the wide swinging doors, but for the smell. It could have also been an aid station in the trenches of France, or an abattoir. Doc Mills kept a spotless morgue, but there wasn't a way to clean the air in which the smells associated with the dead hung like a fog over the river.

"Good afternoon, Inspector," Coroner Mills greeted him. Mills stood at the foot of an exam table in black suit and tie with a crisply-pressed white shirt. He looked more like the next profession in line for a body, an undertaker. His face was pale and virtually expressionless, a trait acquired from years of somberly investigating the causes of death in basement morgues. Beside Mills stood Piper and Timmons.

"Hey, Art," Timmons said, always the friendlier of the pair.

Piper simply nodded his head, smoking a cigarette.

"Doc, Sean, Juan," Treece responded, making the rounds with quick handclasps. "Came to lend some help, fellas, if you'll have me."

"Much obliged, Arthur," the Coroner said.

"So what have your sawbones found so far?"

On the exam table were the mortal remains of Alice

Mallett, without a stitch of clothing on her. Standing above

her body with blood-streaked gloves and aprons, were Dr.

Seybold and Dr. Thomas Hacker who were conducting the

autopsy examination.

"Tom?" Mills prompted.

"A well-nourished female, development consistent

with her reported age of thirty-five years. Right side of her

head was pretty much crushed," Dr. Hacker said, getting

right to the point with no preamble. The light from the

bright lamp above him reflected off his glasses, hiding his

eyes. A white mask tied around his head covered his nose

and mouth. He pointed out his findings with a scalpel as he

went along. "She's got two deeps cuts on the back of her

head here," he said, gingerly rotating the body's head with

his two hands to give Treece a better view. "While deep,

there are no corresponding fractures of the skull."

"As you can see," Dr. Seybold continued, "there are

at least two lacerations across the throat. Deep, they bisected the airway, esophagus, and both the jugular and carotid."

The wounds were gaping red slashes which in part overlapped, combining to form a grotesque second mouth. Fat the color of raw chicken skin gave way to the white and orange muscle planes of the neck.

"The head was nearly severed," Hacker said, centering the head on the table.

"We found an ax at the location where the body was discovered," Piper said, exhaling smoke through his nostrils. The stench, not the sights, is what got to him. The smoldering Camel helped.

"The head wounds would be consistent with an edged, heavy object, such as an ax blade," one of the doctors offered. With their heads down over their work and shoulders hunched, it wasn't always clear who was speaking.

"I've seen more than a few ax wounds in my time here in Michigan," Seybold said, looking up. "The cuts to the throat, however, look too neat to have been caused by anything such as an ax. These cuts are clean, virtually no tearing of the skin or abrasions around them which you'd find with a more blunt edge of an ax or hatchet. I'd say the cuts to the throat were caused by a hunting or butcher's knife, unless it was a new or freshly honed and sharpened ax."

The men gazed at the body for several minutes. Hacker and Seybold seemed to be wrapping up their examination. The incision which had been made down the body's front formed a large "Y" which started at the collar bones, converged at the sternum, and ended at the pubic bone. Now, it was stitched closed with heavy gauge waxed silk in rough crosses, reminding Treece of a burlap potato sack. It was easier to think of it as being something other than the vessel of flesh and bone which was formerly home to a soul.

"Christ, it stinks in here," Timmons finally said. "Let's take Art outside and fill him in on the scoop, Juan."

"Sure thing, Sean." The men walked back out of the exam room and down the hall, Treece's boots clicking and clopping all the way up the stairs. He was pleased to see that his troopers were no longer loitering in the building's lobby.

"Care for a smoke?" Piper asked Treece, who declined. Timmons, again one not to turn down a free one, snatched up the offered cigarette.

"So our guy likes to use an ax, and then a knife for the fine work," Treece offered.

"We figure he felled the woman from behind with the ax, which has got to be the one found at the scene. She was on her way back from having some ice cream with a female friend of hers, some time around 10:30, or so," Piper said. "Our guy caught up with her around Lansing and Jefferson."

"Lansing and Jefferson isn't all the quiet of a corner," Treece said. "No witnesses? With the circus closing shop around that time, there ought to have been a fair piece of traffic in that area. Folks walking around, riding."

"No witnesses. He chops her from behind with the ax, right through her hat, knocks her out, she hits the ground without a sound, dropping her groceries."

"Eggs and flowers," Timmons added, if for no other reason than common curiosity.

"He may have given her another whack to the back of the head with the ax, just to make sure she's out," Piper continued with the more relevant points. "He grabs her up and drags her through a garden that's at the scene. Got some blood in the garden, on the lawn. Takes her across the lawn, closer to the street."

"Why?"

"Don't know, of course, but there's no street lamps there," Piper suggested. "It's further from the house, and under a big tree. While it's closer to the street, the low hanging branches provide more cover."

"That's where he dumped her purse, looking for money, we suppose," said Timmons. "Lot more blood there, so it's where the fella finished the job with a sharp knife like Doc Seybold said. Her coat was off her body and had mopped up a lot of the blood. Her clothes were pretty much torn off. What's that tell us?"

"Tells us he slit her throat first, then ripped open her dress, removed her coat," Treece hypothesized. "Had to have gotten himself covered in blood, cutting her head near off her neck. Any trail of blood to follow?"

"Not much of one," Timmons answered. "There's some leading from where the body was, towards the fairgrounds where the circus was set up. We're bringing in the dogs to see if they can catch a scent. Ought to be there by now."

"We also found a handkerchief under the tree," Piper noted. "It was wadded up and soaked with blood and spit."

"So he conks her on the head, gags her, drags her, and does her in," Treece continued. "He rips her clothes open to look for money, jewelry, and maybe gets a thrill out of stripping her.
No witnesses have turned up, eh?"

"Nope," Piper said. "We got the body identified, but nobody saw anything. The scene's been combed over pretty good for evidence, too. Could be this fella who's been jumping out on women and grabbing them. No real harm done, besides scaring the bejesus out of them. At least until now," he added unnecessarily.

"And in all probability, you've got the ax."

"Yup," Timmons said. "Coroner Mills suggested we put it in the window down at *The Citizen Patriot* offices on South Jackson, see if anybody recognizes it. We're gonna have it put there in the morning. Every available man's out looking for this fiend, but we want to make sure we have an officer at the *Cit-Pat* guarding the ax, so it'll have to wait until the morning. I'm sure that a lot of folks will be by to take a look."

"Even just the curious, I'm sure," Treece said. "Little old biddies who've never wielded so much as a hatchet going by to see. Have you dragged in the usual riff-raff?"

"As we speak," Timmons said. "Sheriff's deputies

are collecting the vagabonds and vagrants."

"What do y'all know about your victim?"

"She's a dead fish on a table," Timmons said.

"Don't let the John Q. Public hear talk like that," Treece admonished. "The papers will have her canonized by the morning edition. Family been contacted?"

"Alice Mallett, thirty-five," Piper said. "A matron at Crittendon, originally from out West, town called Ontario, Oregon, I think. Her brother, Harold Mallett, is making plans to head out here by rail. Probably leave Oregon tomorrow, Northern Pacific to Chicago, and then the Michigan Central. He should be here on Monday evening."

"No local family?"

"Nope, all out West. The brother will be taking the body back to Oregon for burial."

"Enemies? Lovers? Did she have anybody?"

"By all accounts, she just had work," Piper said. "No jealous boyfriend or drunk husband. I think she was just in the wrong place when some fella got the hankering to bump off a woman."

"She was pretty popular with folks who knew her," Timmons added. "In fact, Reverend Griffith is planning a service for Monday."

"What else you know about her?"

"Ada Smith identified her and had more background. Part of some bee's knees pioneer family. Came out here to Michigan about six years past. Worked in Flint and Bay City at the YMCA for three years before settling here."

Deputy Russell Blake of the Jackson County Sheriff's Department came into view around the corner of the county building, a grin appearing on his face behind his bushy mustache when he spotted the lead investigators.

"Heya, Sean," he called, slightly out of breath. His wool uniform was soaked under the arms and between the shoulder blades with sweat from his exertions in the heat of the early afternoon. "The dogs got here from Lansing, caught a scent at the scene and took off down West Madison Street. Towards the fairgrounds and the Robinson Circus."

"They still tracking?" Piper inquired.

"Nah, lost it with all the animal smells at the circus. They've got elephants and all sorts. Plus, they've started pulling up stakes, so it's pretty much a mess there."

"Gonna get some rain through here tonight," Treece said. He was always confident that rainfall was on the way when his trick knee started aching, one more souvenir from the War. "Even if they pick up the trail again, it'll be a sumbitch to follow once it starts pouring."

"Where's the circus headed?" Piper wanted to

know.

"Sandusky," Blake said, referring to an Ohio town on the shores of Lake Erie, about 150 miles away.

"What do you think, Art?" Piper asked, deferring to the more experience inspector.

"Well, you rounded up the vagrants, so someone ought to be questioning them, make sure that they can account for their time last night," Treece said. "I'll get a trooper at my post to send telegrams to the other ones, spread the word about this murder, see if they pick up any possible suspects. Juan, why don't you and I pack a change of clothes and meet the circus in Sandusky?"

"Why not just check out the Circus while it's still here?" Deputy Blake suggested.

"Because, Russ," Piper answered, picking a loose bit of tobacco from the tip of his tongue. "If they are pulling up stakes right now, chances are some of them have already headed out on the Michigan Central or are on the road to Ohio. Even better chances that if our fella is associated with the Circus, he was one of the first to pound sand out of here."

"Let's get some patrols organized for tonight," Timmons said, contributing to the investigative planning. "Maybe he's still on the prowl about town. At least it'll make the folks around here feel better."

"And earn you some more overtime pay, Sean," Piper chided his partner.

"Hey, I took a beating betting on the Philly Athletics last night," Timmons admitted. "Some extra scratch can come in handy."

"That's what you get for putting money down on the visitors," Piper said, leading the group towards the police department.

*****

The evening turned into a wet night as the rains did in fact move in with a cold front off Lake Michigan. Plank bridges over some drainage ditches washed out with localized flash floods, making nighttime travel potentially treacherous. Timmons led a posse of law enforcement officers and civilian volunteers who patrolled the city streets and county roads. By automobile, on horseback, and on foot, the men scoured the area, rousting stumblebums, drunkards, and an assortment of other ne're-do-wells from alleyways, street corners, and vacant structures in the warehouse district along the river. Of those the patrols came across, all were questioned where they were found about their activities the previous evening. Some of the questioning, especially that done by the civilian members of the posse, was aggressive and involved the use of police-issued billy clubs and leather-covered ball bearings. Word among the vagrants spread quickly, and many of these types of the city's uncounted populace soon vacated the area for the rural parts of the county where they were less likely to lose some teeth to a mob acting with impunity. Some of those the patrols did find were taken to the county jail for further questioning. Almost two dozen men were held for further questioning after their initial responses proved unsatisfactory.

There were hounds from Lansing and Mason, baying and wailing as they pulled their leashes taunt, but the scents they picked up on all seemed to lead nowhere. One team of dogs was given a scent from some clothes a man named Barney Love had discovered in the Drexel addition, but that turned into a wild goose chase. As two o'clock in the morning came and passed, the patrols were called off for the remainder of the night. Losing men, dogs, or horses in the wet and dark wouldn't do Alice Mallett any good.

CHAPTER FOUR

Saturday, June 10, 1922

Early Saturday morning, Officer Dean Anderson, an officer with the Kalamazoo City Department of Public Safety, casually strolled into the local State Police post. As he did every morning on the short walk to his beat, Anderson stopped in on the pretenses of visiting a colleague to discuss Volstead Act enforcement. What really brought the city officer to the state post was the fresh coffee his colleagues brewed. The pay with the city wasn't all that great, so Anderson picked up all the freebies he could find, from this coffee he was pouring into a thick porcelain mug, to the frosty beer the proprietor of one of the many speaks on his beat poured for him every afternoon. Having worked the third shift right into the first, his regular tour of duty, the coffee was even better than usual.

Sipping his coffee, Anderson gazed through the steam under his nose at the bulletin board, casually reading postings for community events, farm equipment for sale, and more official announcements. He came upon one which was a telegram from the Michigan Department of State Police post in Jackson, detailing the horrific murder of Alice Mallett. The telegram advised law enforcement officers to be on the lookout for likely suspects, the authorities in Jackson believing the suspect to have fled the area.

Anderson's beat included Botsford Yard, a large railroad yard in the city which would be the site of a major derailment two years later. Just after midnight, having heard shouting from inside a box car, he had rousted a suspicious character from a freight train loaded with Jackson Automobile Company sedans. When Anderson slid open the side door of the car, a young Negro male with blood on his clothes had jumped out of the box car like a jackrabbit, leaping down to the gravel ballast around the tracks.

Anderson had had to chase him clear across the yard to the

big Michigan Central Railroad roundhouse. Anderson put

down his mug and went searching for the post's captain on

the day shift. By eight o'clock that morning, Vern Kutt with

the Jackson County Sheriff's Department was accompanying

Coroner Mills and a newspaper reporter from *The Citizen

Patriot* to Kalamazoo. The three men from Jackson would

be in Kalamazoo by noon.

*****

Detective Juan Piper and Inspector Arthur Treece of

the Michigan Department of State Police spent much of their

Saturday traveling in pursuit of the Robinson Circus. On

Saturday morning, a large group of looky-loos loitered in

front of the *Cit-Pat* windows ogling the bloody ax which

had been recovered from the scene of Alice Mallett's

murder. As predicted, it was more curiosity which drew the

spectators, as none either recognized the tool-turned-weapon, nor had the loss of such an item to report.

"Any bites?" Piper asked the officer guarding the evidence.

"Not a one, Juan," was the answer. The subtle ribbing about his first name never ceased.

When Coroner Mills was satisfied that nothing would come of its viewing, he acquiesced to allowing Treece to take the ax with them to see if attempts at its identification would be more fruitful at the circus in Sandusky.

Trooper Mulbar drove Piper and Treece in his Dodge southeast across the state line to Toledo, Ohio. Referred to at times as Toledo, Michigan, or Michigan's second largest city, in reference to that city's past history as being territory of either Michigan or Ohio, the city had a lot to offer, but they were just passing through. They did, however, grab a bite at the train station, and a breath fo relief. The men were pleased to be out of the sedan and away from Mulbar's wild driving.

"Try not to wrap the Dodge around any trees, Harry," Treece warned. "Unless you want to learn to ride a horse."

The Lake Shore and Michigan Southern Railway which as a teenager Piper would ride with his parents to visit family in Cleveland, was now part of the New York Central Railroad, and it was on those rails which Piper and Treece now traveled east to Sandusky.

Being part of the "Water Level Route" with rails which ran mostly along the flat geography along the Great Lakes from Chicago to New York, the New York Central Railroad used the fast 4-6-4 Hudson steam locomotives on standard gauge tracks. On one hand, this meant a speedy trip. On the other hand, the line was not an express and consequently had frequent stops. The men had a late lunch

in Milbury Junction, coffee in Oak Harbor, and they supped
in Port Clinton.

"This would be an enjoyable leisure trip, Art," Piper
said, relaxing after supper enough to use first names.

"Sure," Treece responded, "if not for the dead fish on
the table back in Jackson."

*****

Vern Kutt towered over the slight frame of Freeman
Hockett, the twenty year-old Negro Officer Anderson had
captured at the MCRR's Botsford yard. Kutt and Mills had
just begun questioning the suspect, a reporter from *The
Jackson Citizen Patriot* sitting in an opposite corner.
Despite the ride from Jackson, neither the undersheriff nor
the coroner had caught the reporter's name. He had simply
been introduced as the crime blotter reporter for the *Cit-Pat*,
who would be granted great access to all portions of the
investigation, due to an agreement between Chief Bean,

Colonel Vandercook, and the newspaper's publisher.

George Gough Booth, who along with his brother was the publisher of *The Jackson Citizen Patriot* and several other newspapers across the southern part of Michigan, agreed that the law enforcement agencies could weigh-in on the timing of publication of certain details of the crime and investigation, provided his paper got the scoop. Related by marriage to E.W. Scripps, and founder of the Cranbrook Educational Community in Bloomfield Hills, Booth knew that exclusivity on a story like this one would be valuable.

Kutt wasn't too keen on having a member of the press in the room for the interrogation, as it would require more talk than brawn. Although, that very same newspaper had just the day before branded the murder of Alice Mallett as an "atrocious crime" and a "dastardly deed," so Kutt thought he might be able to work in a few swats from his blackjack if necessary, without public comment from the press.

Officer Anderson stood along the back wall of the interrogation room, next to the Jackson County coroner.

"What you go by, boy?" Kutt asked, leaning down towards the seated Hockett.

"Blackie Burns is what they call me," Hockett said.

"Okay, Blackie, so where you hail from?"

"Nashville." His answers were short as he kept his head down. Hockett wore no less than three shirts under a scruffy suit jacket, and two pairs of pants, the latest in hobo fashion. It saved a vagabond from the necessity and trouble of a suitcase if he literally carried everything on his body. Hockett's body, and wardrobe, gave off an awful odor.

"Long way from Tennessee," Mills commented. "What brings you through Michigan, Mr. Hockett?"

"Been working in Hammond," he answered, wiping his nose with his multiple sleeves.

"That still ain't Michigan," Kutt said, removing his blackjack from a back pocket. "What kind of work?" Kutt's brute style of questioning conflicted with the coroner's civility, an unintended good cop/bad cop technique.

"Construction."

"What, building a road from Hammond to Kalamazoo?"

"Caught a freight to Detroit," Hockett offered. "Done figured I could catch something heading south from there. Jumped off at Ann Arbor when the train stopped, then got back on."

"And wound up in Kalamazoo?" Kutt asked, his voice heavy with skepticism. "You have a real queer way of heading south. East to Detroit from Indiana, back west to Ann Arbor, then farther west and north to Kalamazoo? That ain't no way to get to Nashville, boy. You got something wrong in that head of yours?"

"No, sir, I ain't got nothing wrong."

"Found him to have a knife on him," Anderson said.

"Any money or a woman's belonging?" Mills asked.

"Just the knife, twenty-seven cents, and all that blood on his clothes."

"Been in a fight with a woman," Hockett said, before the question was asked.

"Looks that way," Kutt said agreeably. "Now would this have been with a woman in Hammond, Detroit, Ann Arbor, or Kalamazoo."

"Cincinnati."

"Oh, ho," Kutt boomed. "Now when in the hell were you in Cincinnati?"

"On my way up from Nashville."

"And you've just been traipsing along for a few weeks, doing a job in Hammond, riding the rails, and that dried blood all over your clothes don't draw no attention from nobody?"

"Guess not," came his feeble response.

"Your blood?"

"I guess."

"He don't have no cuts or anything on his body when we booked him," Anderson said.

"Did you travel through Jackson on your sojourn?" Mills asked.

"I traveled on my feet in the back of a freight. I ain't even know what a so-jurn is."

"Did the train stop in Jackson?"

"Don't know. Don't recall getting off there. I only get off the train when I've got to get some food. Other hobos done take your spot if you get off the train too much. That's how I got stuck in that automobile box car this officer chased me out of," he said, nodding towards Anderson.

"Better roll down the windows on the Ford," Kutt said, "because we're taking this sumbitch back to Jackson with us."

*****

Treece and Piper arrived at the fairgrounds in Sandusky at dusk, having been escorted by members of the local constabulary to the location where the John Robinson Circus set up the latest stop. The banners proclaimed that this was their 99th Annual Tour. The Michigan investigators took some time getting nickel cotton candy and taking in the sights.

The circus mascot on the banners and sides of the circus train's box cars was a red-cheeked clown, promising "everlastingly good" attractions for the price of admission. In the pictures, the clown was typically flanked by scantily-dressed young women, who were in either their undergarments or swimming suits, Piper couldn't quite tell.

City police rounded up workers of the circus and detained them in an area near the rail cars for questioning, the vast majority of them being Negro.

"We'll give these fellas some questions," Treece explained to the Sandusky sergeant in charge, a squat, older man named Clark. "We'd appreciate it if you and your men would check out the sleeping cars and the property of these men. Foot lockers, suitcases, whatever they've got their belongings stuffed into."

"Anything specific you're looking for," the sergeant asked.

"Anything soiled with blood, for the most part," Piper said. "Our victim was cut and chopped pretty good, we figure the perpetrator got himself messy. From the looks of the circus employees, it doesn't look like they get a lot of chances to catch a bath or launder their clothes."

"Y'all figure it's one of these coloreds from the

circus?"

"Well, I'll leave that to your deductive skills of reason as an investigator," Treece said.

The questioning was laborious, the interviewees less than cooperative at first, and perhaps rightly so. It was hard enough to get a job as a Negro, even in the North. The pre-World War Two boom of the automobile and aircraft industry, when Southern Michigan became the "Arsenal of Democracy," was still nearly twenty years off. Some prosperity and job security would arrive with Henry Ford's promise of a top-paying assembly job at River Rouge or making B-24 Liberty bombers at Willow Run. Until then, there were few opportunities beside back-breaking crop harvesting in the fields. The tasks were still primarily demanding physical labor, raising tent poles, loading rail cars, shoveling the droppings from Old Pitt, one of the four "Military Elephants" who performed a skit in uniforms, but the John Robinson Circus let these men travel the country,

sleeping in warm quarters with full bellies.

But the benefits of the job created a dichotomy of

feelings in these men when rousted by the authorities. On

one hand, it was just another hassle and harassment they had

to endure, being questioned just because somebody down

the line pointed the finger for a white woman's murder at a

black man, and they kept their answers short and curt.

However, the benefits of the job also engendered mistrust if

any of them committed any act which might threaten their

relatively good thing. It was that sentiment which cause

several of the men, as Piper and Treece questioned them one

at a time in the train's dining car, to give them a viable

suspect.

"Clark Meadowlark," Treece said when grouped

back with Sergeant Clark, the other Sandusky officers, and

Juan Piper. "Cook with the Circus up until the stop in

Jackson. His former co-workers say that Meadowlark got fired for ogling too many of the female patrons."

"That sounds promising," the sergeant said.

"The other men say that they heard Meadowlark say some threatening things," Piper added, "and that he'd meet up with the circus in Painesville. Said he'd be there to collect his wages, one way or another."

"Any of them identify that ax?" Clark asked.

"No," Treece said. They were as of yet unable to firmly establish that the ax they had brought with them, which had so far traveled from the murder scene outside Robert Brockie's house to the front window at the *Cit-Pat*, and then here to Sandusky, Ohio, was the property of the John Robinson Circus.

The investigators dined on greasy carnival food and beer while catching some acts under the big top. The supposed "Strongest Man on Earth," Louis Cyr, assisted by

"The French Hercules" Horace Barre, entertained the audience with their weight-lifting feats. Cyr would shoulder a plank of wood with nearly a dozen men standing atop it, while Barre strained under the bulk of a young elephant. The spectacle reminded both Treece and Piper why they did not run to catch the performances when the Circus was in Jackson.

After their dinner, Piper and Treece went to the Sandusky police headquarters and attempted to reach Jackson by telephone. There had been an agreement that communications would be funneled through the county, instead of the Jackson City Police Department or a Michigan Department State Police post. A deputy at the Jackson County Sheriff's Department took the call at the switchboard.

"This is Inspector Treece and Detective Piper," Treece said loudly into the candlestick. "What was that?

Repeat that. What?" The words from the deputy in Jackson came out garbled, tinny, and drowned in static. Treece's words were undoubtedly unintelligible on the deputy's end, as well.

"This isn't going to work," he finally concluded. "Sergeant, can you get a telegram sent for me?"

"Sure," Clark said. "I'll have one of my boys run it down to the railroad station."

"Good," Treece said. He took a piece of paper from a nearby desk and scribbled the message with a pencil.

To: Jackson County Sheriff, Jackson, Michigan. From: Inspector Treece; Detective Piper. Message: Mallett murder suspect identified. Stop. Detach Detective Timmons, two other officers to Painesville, Ohio. Stop. Meet Treece, Piper. Stop. Arrest Circus Cook Clark Meadowlark. Stop.

Clark took the piece of paper into another room at

the front of the station. The murmur of his instructions ended, followed by the ringing of a bell attached above the door. The bell then rang again, indicating the entrance of another person.

"Sergeant Clark," an excited voice said. Piper followed Treece out to the front room.

"What is it, Keane?" the sergeant asked.

"Found these under a mattress in the sleeping car of the circus train," the officer said, breathless from having sprinted from the fairgrounds to the station. In his hands he held a pair of denim overalls, smeared with blood. "Got a handful of bloody handkerchiefs in the pockets."

"They got assigned bedding on that train?" Treece asked.

"Sure do," Officer Keane said.

"Show us," Piper instructed. His pulse was beginning to quicken, like when hunting pheasant and his dogs would go on point just before the flush. After the drudgery of asking the same questions repeatedly and getting useless answers, he was excited for a development.

*****

Det. Harry Collins was a big Irishman, with beefy mitts he could easily wrap around a smaller man's throat. That ability came in handy at times such as these. Collins was a bruiser, and an avid admirer of Jack Britton, Benny Leonard, and other fighters of the day. He even made arrangements with Ike Kantlehner to import a copy of *The London Times* so that he could read about Sunday night's Light-Heavyweight title bout in London between Ted Kid Lewis and Georges Carpentier. Ike sold diamonds and watches, and imported much of his items from Great Britain. It would be no big feat to have a copy of the paper tossed in with the next shipment. Collins was, contrary to his appearance, also in possession of a keen intellect and sharp investigator's mind. That combination garnered him the position of leading the current questioning.

Almost two dozen men had been rounded up since Friday, primarily hobos from the rail yards, vagrants from the soup kitchens, and common hoodlums found on the streets. Specifically, they were those who did not have readily available alibis or accountings for their whereabouts when someone was taking an ax to Alice Mallett like they were felling an oak. Collins and Deputy Russell Blake had arrested Straub when they came upon him Saturday night.

"He might have been drinking," the department's chemist Peter Keyzer advised Collins before leaving the room.

"How recently?"

"His pupils are a bit dilated, so I think he was drunk within the last forty-eight hours."

"But he's sober now?"

"Plenty sober," Keyzer said, walking out of the room and shutting the door behind him.

"Alrighty, George," Collins said to the man seated across the table from him, "what have you been up to since Thursday evening?"

George Straub sat quietly, picking at the cuffs of a stripped inmate shirt with his left hand. Finding blood on his clothes, Collins had had them taken and secured as potential evidence. Straub was in his late forties, but could have passed for much older, with dark brown hair and a weathered face from working outdoors as a laborer. His seated position was stooped, as if weighed down by a yoke. Even though his right hand was virtually crippled from having accidentally cut tendons and nerves while working a job, he looked strong and fit. He was a lifelong Michigander, having been born in Allegan County and never leaving the state.

"Nothing in particular," he answered. "Catch a bite at that Lutheran mission downtown."

"Done time, huh?" Collins commented. "When they fingerprinted you and took your measurements, you said you done time. How much?"

"Six years," Straub answered. "Six years right here at the Jackson pen. Got out in '07."

"You on parole, George?"

"No, I done straight time, full six." From under a protruding brow, Straub squinted his blue eyes at Collins "Got my suit of clothes you done took from me, and my five dollars from the warden, and went about my business." Straub rolled his sleeves up while he spoke.

"Didn't get a real job, though, huh, George?"

"Odd jobs, mostly."

"The warden gave you a train ticket, too, didn't he? Law says you've got to take that ticket and use it, go to some other part of the state and become somebody else's chore, ain't that right, George?"

"I prefer Jackson," Straub said, absently rubbing his accident scar on his right wrist.

"Law says if you don't use that train ticket, you can be locked up for a misdemeanor."

"Law says lots of stuff," Straub responded, showing some convict backbone.

"Yeah, George," Collins said, moving closer. "Law also said that you owed the state six years for statutory rape in Osceola County. A thirteen year-old girl." After being picked up with the other vagrants, Straub had given some information about his past. Collins had had some calls made to check the records at the prison in town, and came up with some choice details.

"Been picked up plenty of times for being drunk and disorderly, George, huh? September of '17 you got picked up right here in Jackson."

"What of it?"

"What 'odd jobs' you been working currently?" Collins asked, deftly controlling the conversation.

"Road crew working on a stretch out past my house on Seymour Avenue," he answered.

"How'd you get that gimpy hand, George."

"I used to work lumber camps, cut it bad one time."

At this point, Collins was aware that investigators had a suspect in Kalamazoo, and another Negro Treece and Piper were going after in Ohio, so he didn't think much of Straub as a suspect. In the interest of being thorough, however, all the vagrants brought in were getting the third degree, regardless of the sentiment that one of the Negro men was the murderer. Collins was about to cut George Straub loose, at least until Straub's last response, which demanded a follow-up question.

"You good with an ax, George?"

*****

Detective Sean Timmons, the anonymous reporter from *The Citizen Patriot*, and two uniformed City of Jackson police officers received the telegram from Treece Saturday night. Officer Cliff Hockman transported the men in his trusty police wagon the ninety miles southeast to Toledo, Ohio. In Toledo, they sat around the station awaiting the arrival of the midnight train which would get them to Painesville Sunday morning.

Timmons didn't quite know what to think as he chain-smoked cigarettes he pilfered from the reporter's luggage when the man went to make a call back to the paper. Kutt and Mills had been grilling a suspect in Kalamazoo, and now his partner and Art Treece were on the prowl for a suspect in Ohio. Well, a slow train smoking free Gitanes wasn't too bad of a way to spend a Saturday night.

The Jackson newspaper, which had editorialized that "every resource of human energy and public finance should be placed behind this effort" to apprehend Alice Mallett's murderer, had covered the cost of tickets for the sleeper car on the train, so the travel would be comfortable, too. The detective's wife wasn't too pleased with his recent late hours and now overnight travel, but the overtime compensation would buy some pretty flowers to smooth thing over. Maybe Timmons would even pick up some perfume and face powder his wife had been eyeing at Van Marter's on West Pearl.

Timmons coughed and hacked, the smoke aggravating a chest cold he guessed he had acquired while leading a posse through the rain the other night.

"You ought to cut down on the smoking," the newspaper man said, returning to the bench at the railroad terminal. "You ought to try my brand. French things, I get from Windsor. Easier on the lungs, they say."

Timmons wiped spittle from his lips which were curving up into a smile, amused with the sight of the reporter searching his bags for his missing cigarettes.

CHAPTER FIVE

Sunday, June 11, 1922

After Timmons had left with others to catch the train in Toledo the night before, Undersheriff Kutt and Coroner Mills brought in their suspect from Kalamazoo.

Freeman "Blackie Burns" Hockett maintained his assertion that the blood on his clothing was the result of a tussle with a long-nailed female in Cincinnati. Despite a spirited interrogation which continued in Jackson at the county jail, Hockett remained steadfast in his claims of innocence in the Mallett affair.

Unable to confirm the supposed alibi, but also unable to obtain any hard evidence that Hockett was involved in Alice Mallett's murder, Kutt stuck the man in a holding cell to cool his heels. Calls were placed to the authorities in Cincinnati, requesting that they locate the woman whom

Hockett claimed to be the source of the blood on his clothing, but they were still checking. The woman may have been a prostitute who worked that city's pig slaughterhouse district, and finding a particular whore in Porkopolis would take some time. Like the men working the John Robinson Circus, Hockett was assured a dry cot and a hot supper, so other than a few bumps and bruises from the questioning, he was relatively better off than being locked in an automobile freight train. Sunday morning, Hockett ate his oatmeal and awaited his eventual release.

In Painesville, Treece and Piper were met by Timmons, the newspaper reporter, and two other officers. Locating the former circus cook, Clark Meadowlark, was fairly simple. They found the man in a shouting match with the paymaster, demanding back wages up until his firing from the circus in Jackson.

"You done got work out of me," Meadowlark was

yelling, "now you all got to give me my pay."

"Keep making demands, Clark," the payroll clerk threatened, "and I'll ask Cyr and Barre to grab you by the arms and make a wish."

"You want to have a go at him?" Treece asked Timmons.

"It would be nice to actually do something other than ride around seeing the Great Lakes by train."

The uniformed Jackson officers pounced on Meadowlark, wrestling him to the ground and placing ratchet handcuffs on his wrists.

By the scruff of his neck, hands behind his back, Meadowlark was directed up a wooden pallet by Timmons, into one of the passenger rail cars. Timmons was followed by Piper, and stopped at the first compartment door they came to on the right. The name Abe Goldstein was painted below the glass of the door, indicating the performer's presence with the circus to be more than the transient laborers and their grease pencil-marked bunks. Timmons rapped on the door. A flash of white appeared briefly through velvet drapes on the other side of the glass.

"Yes," a man said, opening the door and causing Timmons to take a slight step back, Meadowlark still in his grip. "May I help you?" the man asked. His face was covered in white powder with vibrant red circles painted on his cheeks and nose. He wore a blue wool constable's uniform complete with bowler resting atop of wig or red hair.

"That's just Abe," Meadowlark spoke for the first time after having been arrested. "Just a damn fool clown."

"And that is the ever-quarrelsome Clark Meadowlark," the clown said. "Just a cook. But he makes a respectable chicken fried steak. Where have you been, Clark? We've had to settle for pork and beans and last couple meals."

"Got to use your compartment," Piper said, ending this absurd dialog between their suspect and a clown.

"Just keep your eyes on him," Goldstein said. "I've got some rabbits I use in my act which Clark here always coveted for his kitchen pot." The clown left and from a paper sack he had been carrying, Piper pulled out a bloodied pair of overalls.

"Leave something behind when you got canned?" Piper asked, beginning the questioning.

There was some coaxing, but when a handkerchief was found on Meadowlark's person which matched the ones soaked in blood from the overalls, the suspect admitted that the overalls were his. He did not, however, care to explain the presence of blood. On the trousers Meadowlark wore, there appeared to be more staining of dried blood.

While the detectives questioned Meadowlark in the

clown's quarters, Treece continued walking about the circus

with the ax wrapped, appropriately enough, in butcher's

paper. He would remove the item out of the brown paper to

show to circus employees, but none acknowledged

ownership nor the ability to identify it as property of the

circus. In his boots and hat, some of the circus patrons

thought he was part of a Buffalo Bill revival and asked

where Annie Oakley was shooting.

Late in the day, Treece and Piper conferred on the

investigation while Timmons, the newspaper man, and the

other two officers headed off to the train station to transport

Meadowlark back to Jackson for further questioning. They

had also sent the overalls back with Timmons so that the

department's chemist, Peter Keyzer, could look them over.

"Nobody recalls using this ax, seeing it, tripping over

it, nothing," Treece told Piper, shaking the item in its

wrappings for emphasis. "Meadowlark is linked to the

circus, but if we can't place the ax with the circus, we can't put it in his hands."

"What about the bloody overalls and handkerchiefs?" Piper asked. "He doesn't have an explanation for them."

"He might, but he isn't telling, either. And he doesn't need one," Treece said, feeling weary from the long and so far unproductive hours. "Bloody clothes under the bed aren't a crime, far as I can tell. You know of some ordnance or state statute that I don't?"

"Did you run that ax by everybody?" Piper asked, ignoring the rhetorical question.

"Not yet," Treece said, pulling out a box of cigarettes and some wooden matches. "That partner of yours is gone, so I figure it's safe to light up," he said, extending the items to Piper, who chuckled.

"Not much gets by you, huh?"

"I'm just an old horse soldier," Treece said, "but my eyes still work pretty well. Do you know where this train of animals and freaks is off to next?"

"Warren," Piper said. "When we were done with Meadowlark, I asked that clown some questions. Seems they stay a couple days in the bigger towns, but barely twenty-four hours in the smaller places like here in Painesville. They start packing before the last crack of the lion tamer's whip. The clown offered to share his compartment. Fifteen years on the road with this shebang and his seniority gets him the bigger quarters."

"Well, let's ride it out to Warren, then," Treece said. "It'll give us another day to ask about the ax. Maybe come up with more suspects."

"You don't think the cook is our man, do you?"

"Don't know, at least not yet," Treece answered, a sigh sending smoke into the air. "I'm thinking that a Negro walking the streets of Jackson with an ax slung over his shoulder is probably going to get some attention. Lord knows that there are enough white sheets hanging up in the back of closets that he wouldn't have gotten far."

"Who, then?" Piper asked. "And why? Robbery?"

"Maybe, at least initially," Treece said. "But you just knock somebody over the head if you want their money. You don't hack and slash and then tear off your mark's clothing."

"So?"

"So, whoever chopped down Alice Mallett may have liked doing it. And what do you do when you find something you like doing?"

"Keep doing it," Piper answered, his throat clicking audibly when he swallowed.

Just dry from smoking, he lied to himself, trying to keep the thought out of his mind that there was a very real possibility that if they didn't find this guy, they would be

finding another body or two on the city's streets.

CHAPTER SIX

Monday, June 12, 1922

As far as Inspector Art Treece and Detective Juan Piper were concerned, the investigation was no further along that it had been Friday morning. Technically, it was progressing, as eliminating suspects was useful. But the investigators didn't care to know who *didn't* do it; they wanted to know who *did* do it. Today was only the beginning of the fourth day of the investigation, but they were nevertheless getting frustrated with the pace.

Before returning to Jackson, they had worked over the circus workers once more that morning in Warren, Ohio. Unable to positively identify the likely murder weapon as property of the John Robinson Circus, the evidence against Clark Meadowlark wasn't materializing.

Peter Keyzer, the Jackson Police Department's

chemist, found the supposed blood on Meadowlark's trousers to actually be staining left by a bar of Lava soap he carried around with him. Often dragged from his kitchen to assist the other circus laborers in tasks such as shoveling manure out of the horse car compartments, a bar of soap was indispensable to the cook. Keyzer notified the investigators by telephone of his findings.

"These leads," Piper commented while he and Treece were in Warren, Ohio, "are a load of heifer dust. You get that feeling?"

"You asking me if I'm thinking of railroading some colored boy for this?"

"Something like that."

"You know what I like, Juan?" Treece asked. "I like sitting on my porch, sipping some rye, watching my horses graze and my dogs tromp around the tall grass, sniffing up morning doves and rabbits. Running around the country putting my riding boots in elephant dung ain't even a close second to that." Treece was agitated with the state of the investigation, and his ire was up. "What would you rather be doing, Juan? Having a drink on the porch, or framing up some random fellow on account of his skin color just to get in good with the city manager and your Chief Bean?"

"Point taken," Piper said.

The investigators did develop other suspects, focusing their general suspicions on the basis that the perpetrator was a Negro associated with the circus. There were numerous tips and leads reported by the public, but none proved verifiable nor ultimately credible.

A boy ten years old had a ludicrous claim of having witnessed the murder. Little Angelo Glalanelly said that he saw with his own eyes a black man in pursuit of the victim, with the suspected weapon in his hands. The discovery of newspaper clippings covering the murder in young Angelo's bedroom by his mother led to his story being discredited, and a sore behind from the leather of his father's belt.

Back in Jackson, Officer Mulbar was granted a reprieve from tracking down the fugitive Potawatomi Little Bear Smith so that he could assist in hearing the suspicions of citizens. If they were looking for some fellow with loose marbles rolling around in his head, Mulbar did not think that these complainants were much more in control of their faculties. Neighbors named each other as the Mallett killer, for no other reason than a long-running feud or past slight.

When Lottie Baginsky stopped by the state police post, she claimed that Herme Davis was the perpetrator. On Thursday, June 8th, Mrs. Baginsky alleged that Davis had come to the side door of her home on Adams Street no fewer than three times seeking employment to fix a broken porch rail. She further claimed to have seen the wooden handle of an ax under his coat.

"At least three times," she told a sympathetic-looking Officer Mulbar. After a few hours of this, he had perfected the look, hiding his disbelief. Maybe looking for some crazy Indian in the woods wasn't so bad, he thought.

"I told him, 'No, thank you. Mr. Baginsky is more than capable of fixing the rail.' That's exactly as I put it to him," Mrs. Baginsky explained.

"Yes, ma'am," Mulbar muttered, his chin resting in a hand while he sat at a desk across from the complainant, doodling with a pencil. "Could it have been a hammer or handle of another tool you saw him in possession of?"

"No, it had to be an ax. And it had nothing to do with him being a Negro," she added defensively. "He's got such fair skin, anyway, I didn't realize he was until later."

"Yes, ma'am. And have you read about this murder in the newspapers?"

"Oh, yes, young man," she answered brightly. "I've

read every line of copy, and have probably memorized every detail." Mulbar thought that Baginsky's reading of the final home edition of the newspaper before bed each night was the probable source of her "recollection" of seeing Davis with an ax. Nevertheless, they would check it out. He wrote down some notes and passed it off to the day shift desk sergeant who would forward the information to the Jackson Police Department detectives and the Michigan State Police.

Davis had been picked up loitering in a Jackson railroad yard during the roundup of vagrants late Friday, so he was already in custody when Mrs. Baginsky made her allegations.

Sean Timmons and the two Jackson officers who had accompanied him to Ohio to arrest Clark Meadowlark had returned to the city late the previous night, their prisoner in tow.

Meadowlark was placed in a line-up at the county

jail along with Davis and four other black men. Lottie Baginsky stood with Mulbar in an adjoining, darkened room, looking through a peephole in the wall so that those standing under the lights could not see the witnesses.

"That's the one," Baginsky said. "The light-skinned one, at the far right." She spoke in a whisper, as if the men in the line-up would be able to hear her through the wall. She identified Herme Davis.

The identification cast doubt on Clark Meadowlark's guilt, as he was much darker than Davis, with skin the color of cocoa. However, the cook from the circus would remain in custody, at least for the time being.

Timmons conducted further questioning of Davis, leaning on him hard, but having the same doubts as Mulbar about Baginsky's credibility as a witness.

"Thursday night, why'd you go and do a thing like chop up a God-fearing, church-going woman?"

"What? Where? When?" Davis responded.

"Murder. Jackson. Thursday night."

"Uh-uh, sir," Davis protested, sweating heavily.

Timmons didn't like to see suspects sweat. First, it stunk up the interview rooms and stained the chairs. Secondly, and more importantly, the innocent were the ones who sweated up their clothes, nervous as an eight-point buck on the opening day of hunting season.

"I didn't even get into town until near midnight on Friday," Davis explained. That was over twenty-four hours beyond the probable time of the murder Thursday night. "I came in from Michigan City, by way of Niles. I done had two friends with me, too."

The two friends were fellow vagabonds passing through, and had also been picked up by one of the patrols the other night. The group of detectives who questioned them believed the alibi to be truthful. The stories of all three matched in all of the important details, and with prejudices of the day, two white men, as were the traveling companions of Davis, vouching for a black man carried an awful lot of weight.

*****

Charlie Jackson, as Joseph Evens liked to be called, was one of the few suspects who was not a Negro, and perhaps that was why Inspector Treece and Detective Piper looked him over with an especially keen eye. The investigators were still with the John Robinson Circus at its engagement in Warren, Ohio, and were still grilling employees when they received the suspicions of a restaurant owner named Ernest Cote. The information had been telegraphed from Jackson to Warren. Treece and Piper asked around the circus before grabbing Jackson for questioning.

Charlie Jackson was an odd duck to begin with,

garnering suspicion immediately. He was a scrawny white male who had taken bleach to his hair to make it yellowish-white in color, like sickly corn silk left to rot on the stalk after the frost. He had been a Jackson resident before joining the circus life about a year or so before, first with the Hagenbach-Wallace Circus as an elephant handler and rider. Earlier this year, Jackson joined the John Robinson Circus for slightly more pay and a better position as a clown and occasional ticket seller. It was definitely a better position, he explained while telling his life's story to the detectives, than having to ride the elephants, putting up with the dust and smell.

"What did you do before the circus work?" Piper asked. They had commandeered Abe Goldstein's train compartment once again to use as a private interview room. Again, the clown warned the investigators to look after his rabbits.

"Old Charlie there is known to jump on just about anything, woman, man, or beast," Goldstein explained. "I don't care to have my rabbits cooked by the likes of Clark, nor abused at the hands of Charlie."

"I sold insurance in Jackson at Berger Insurance in the Dwight Building, and worked as a cook at the American Grill on South Mechanic." He brushed a lock of hair from his forehead, revealing darker strands and roots beneath.

"So what's the rest of the story?" Piper asked. He and Treece stood in front of a seated Charlie Jackson, a fold-down desk coming out of the wall. Piper dumped the contents of a burlap sack onto the desk. These interrogations were beginning to feel like elementary school show-and-tell.

"This came from your sleeping quarters," Piper said, referring to a hard leather case which had fallen from the bag. There appeared to be blood on the outside of the case, which he pried open. Inside were women's grooming instruments. Two pairs of reading glasses, also women's from their design, rested beside the case on the desk top.

"I use those things for my performance," Jackson said.

"Tweezers, brushes," Treece said, going through the case. "You some sort of nancy boy, plucking your eyebrows?"

"The white face paint," Jackson began to explain. "It dries like cement in my eyebrows. If I don't keep them bare, it's a might painful effort to get all the paint off."

"What's with the blood on the case, Charlie?" Piper asked pointedly, leaning forward.

"Cut myself shaving."

"Funny, we didn't find any razor in that case, Charlie."

"Someone must have lifted it," Jackson said. "This

circus is rife with kleptomaniacs and thieves."

"Among other types," Treece added.

"Found some queer stuff in your suitcase," Piper said. "Nudie books part of your clown act, too? Silk stockings, colorful handkerchiefs? You one of them queers, Charlie?"

The beat red color which rose up in Jackson's cheeks would have taken quite a bit of white face paint to hide.

"What you doing in your spare time, Charlie?" Treece asked, working in more facts they had learned about Jackson before the interview. "You like to go to the park and relax?"

"Sure," Jackson answered. "Who don't like that?"

"Well," Piper jumped in, "most folks might like sitting on a bench feeding the birds. But most folks, at least the men, don't sneak into the women's toilets."

"I just walked into the wrong one," Jackson

responded quickly.

"And playing in your trousers while in there," Treece added. The information the investigators had gathered included a story that just the previous day, Jackson had been discovered in a public park just outside of Warren, in the ladies toilet. A group of local men had dragged him out and had meant to do Jackson bodily harm before he managed to escape their wrath and catch a bus back to the circus grounds.

They continued questioning Jackson for hours, rotating in some detectives from the local police so that Piper and Treece could take a break from time to time. By late that evening, they had not established Jackson's guilt in the Mallett murder, but had reached a conclusion that Jackson was a moral degenerate who ought to be held in the local jail and off the streets for as long as possible. He was another one who would be taken back to Jackson, Michigan.

Not only did their suspicions that the killer was a circus employee fail to become fact, the belief that the ax was circus property also began to wane. Of the workers who were questioned, none were able to identify the ax. The management, who had been fairly cooperative with the investigations, began to show their aggravation with their employees being taken from their arduous, daily tasks, to answer the questions of the detectives. The chief equipment manager for the circus explained that all of the axes used to chop wood, and sledgehammers to pound in tent stakes, had all been replaced with new equipment the previous year. The stains on, and gouges and nicks in, the alleged murder weapon showed the item to be much older. Treece still had his suspicions that the ax had come from the circus, so he generally dismissed the protests of the circus managers as them wanting to be done with the meddling and questioning by the detectives.

Again exhausted from asking endless questions,

Treece and Piper collected their things and accepted a ride

from a Warren officer back to the railroad station in

Sandusky. A train to Toledo and then a ride in Cliff

Hockman's police patrol wagon would get the men back into

their own beds some time Tuesday morning. Figuring that

not much was developing, they both planned to sleep late.

*****

Monday evening, at quarter past six, Harold Mallett

clambered down the steel stairs of his passenger car on the

Michigan Central train he'd been on since Chicago.

Reporters from both *The Citizen Patriot* and *The Jackson*

News, knowing about Mallett's pending arrival, pounced on

the man as his feet hit the boardwalk outside the station.

Rumors made their way around town that there were even a

flock of correspondents from the Associated Press taking up

all of the available boardinghouse rooms.

"Mr. Mallett," a reporter moved in, getting Alice Mallett's brother to pause just long enough for his photographer to shoot a picture with a Kodak Brownie. "What do you say?"

"Justice," Mallett said. "The beast who killed my sister, he needs to receive justice. And that's all I've got to say." The long trip and reason for it weighed heavily on him, as evident in his drained complexion, slowed movement, and curt response. Mallett had left Oregon on Saturday afternoon, and but for changing rail lines from the Northern Pacific to the Michigan Central in Chicago, he'd been sitting in a private compartment, alone with his grief and thoughts. With that, suitcases in hand, Mallett pushed his way past the reporters and spectators towards the street. A representative from the Gildersleeve funeral home, the undertakers contracted to handle arrangements to get Alice Mallett's body back to Ontario, Oregon, took Harold

Mallett by the elbow and directed him towards an awaiting Dodge. Detective Timmons followed in a Model T, blocking out the automobiles of some of the more ardent reporters who began a futile pursuit. After forcing one into a drainage ditch, Timmons watched in the mirror as the other "vultures" slowed to a stop. The two vehicles of the impromptu caravan rushed off towards South Jackson Street and the funeral home.

Reverend Griffith was present upon their arrival at the Gildersleeve funeral home, dressed in black suit and clerical collar. Griffith was getting on in years, rail-thin, his body having previously been ravished by a bout of yellow fever from his time doing missionary work in Cuba. He offered his condolences to Mr. Mallett and remained in the foyer as the mourner was led towards the small chapel at the rear of the establishment.

"Sean," Shannon Griffith said to Timmons, shaking

his hand. "Didn't see you at services this Sunday past." His ministry was at the First Presbyterian Church, of which Timmons was an occasional congregant.

"Sorry about that, Reverend Griffith," Timmons said. "Figured I was doing the Lord's work, trying to find the fella who done bumped off poor Ms. Mallett." While respectful, Timmons had known Griffith long enough to push back a bit.

"Sure," Griffith said. "Come for the service?"

"Yeah," Timmons answered, wishing he had waited to enter the funeral home until after having the last of the cigarettes he'd lifted from that reporter. It reminded him of another item to confess at a later date.

About two dozen people showed up for the service, including the city manager and a half-dozen women from the Florence Crittendon Home. Both those who attended and many who could not provided an abundance of flowers.

Timmons fell in line at the conclusion and offered his own

condolences to Harold Mallett.

"Long trip out here, huh?" Timmons said after

introducing himself.

"Over sixty hours, most of it sitting on a train,"

Mallett responded. "I'm a rancher, Detective Timmons.

Come from a long line of ranchers and pioneers. Can't say

I'm too fond of being cooped-up on a train with nothing to

do but think of my sister." As Timmons had been the last in

line, and Reverend Griffith had bid farewell to go prepare

for vespers, they found themselves alone in the chapel, save

for the closed casket. "So I'll ask the obvious, Timmons.

You catch the fiend yet?"

"You seem like a down-to-earth, brass tacks sort of

man, being a rancher and all," Timmons explained. "So I

ain't gonna feed you any malarkey. We've got some

suspects being held and questioned, every man in the field,

but I can't tell you who done it. Yet."

"Fair enough," the man responded. "I'll take your best effort, can't ask for more."

"We do what we can, Mr. Mallett."

"Hacked her up something awful," Mallett said, looked over his shoulder in the direction of the polished wooden casket. "We slaughter our cattle with more respect than what was done to my sister."

"We've got some things on our side of solving this," Timmons offered, sensing the dejectedness of Harold Mallett. "This here is a fairly small town, not much, and not many, go unnoticed. Somebody's gonna turn up who saw something. For all we know, we've got the guy locked up right now, just a matter of time before he confesses."

"How can I help?"

"We figured you ought to get a good night's sleep, then we'll have some questions for you," Timmons explained. "Reverend Griffith made arrangements for you with Dr. Hendricks to stay at his house on West Cortland. I'll take you over there when you're finished paying your respects. Tomorrow, State Police will be by to ask questions along with a deputy and some city detectives. We're all working together for a change to get Alice her justice," he said, harking back to Harold Mallett's comments to the reporters.

"That's most kind of you and the Reverend," Mallett said. "I'll need to collect Alice's possessions to ship back to Oregon."

"You met Ada Smith, right? She'll make sure all of your sister's things are packed up at Crittendon Home. They'll keep your sister here in their morgue until you're ready to take her."

"Much obliged, Detective Timmons." The detective turned to leave, briefly watching Mallett slump in a chair and light a Camel. Timmons could hear him muttering the

word "justice" more than once.

CHAPTER SEVEN

Tuesday Morning, June 13, 1922

Russell Blake, a deputy with the Jackson County

Sheriff's Department, was alternating his attention from the

bright moon which was just a day or two past being full, and

his Hamilton pocket watch which told him it was almost

three in the morning. He was waiting on Harry Collins with

the Michigan State Police, who had run into the Jackson

MDSP post to grab some flashlights. At two ticks past the

hour, Collins rushed out, a flashlight in each hand.

"Couldn't get something less noticeable?" Collins

asked, referring to the vehicle Blake was driving. It was a

3/4 ton Red Baby pickup truck made by International

Harvester. The hood and cab of the pickup was the color of

a fire engine, with whitewall tires and red wheels which

matched the cab. The bed of the truck was polished wood,

with the McCormick-Deering logo painted in the same red. The truck was built and distributed for the purpose of traversing the United States to provide parts and service for farmers who owned McCormick-Deering tractors.

"Borrowed it from my brother," Blake said. "The county is short of vehicles, so unless you all wanted to ride horseback, not much choice. Besides, why do you think we're skulking around in the middle of the night? We're like that Count Orlok in that *Nosferatu* movie."

"Haven't seen it," Collins said. "Took the wife to see *The Cabinet of Dr. Caligari* and she still makes me leave a lantern lit in the hallway at night. Damned moving pictures." Collins checked to make sure that the flashlights worked. "Ah, doesn't matter. The others can ride in the bed with our suspect."

"Good," Blake said. "This guy done what you think he done, I don't want him riding up here with me. But they better hold on, this'll do thirty miles per hour when it gets going."

"Well, head on over to the jail and let's get this show on the road."

A short time later, the men were greeted at the jail by fellow state troopers Van Loomis and the over-worked Harold Mulbar, as well as Vern Kutt.

"Nice truck," Loomis chided his colleague outside the entrance. "I thought we wanted to be inconspicuous doing this so those damn fool reporters don't jump the gun." Booth's man was being purposely excluded from this particular outing.

"That's why we're skulking around in the middle of the night," Collins said, winking at Deputy Blake and their private joke.

"Let me drag this Straub out here already," Vern Kutt suggested, "before the sun catches up with us. We ought to get him back here before folks start walking to work at sunrise."

"Yep," Office Mulbar contributed to the discussion. "The way folks are sounding that I've talked to, if they think we've got the murderer in custody, they're liable to drag him out to an oak and lynch him on the spot." Vigilante mobs were not something they would want to deal with, especially since the officers would be sympathetic to such a mob's goals.

Besides their general suspicions of Straub from the interview Collins had conducted, there had been a statement from one of Robert Brockie's neighbors indicating that Straub had been seen in the area of Lansing Avenue and Jefferson Street Thursday night. Additionally, Collins had re-interviewed Martha Quick and the other young women who had been accosted by an unknown assailant within the last couple weeks. Their descriptions contained some peculiar physical features which matched those possessed by George Straub. Other women called the State Police post and the Sheriff's Department to detail similar assaults which had previously gone unreported. Those reports as well contained descriptions matching Straub. Mass hysteria was not ruled out, but the reports were promising.

Straub's face was frozen in squinting terror as he was brought out the rear exit of the jail against the headlights of the Red Baby. Collins added to the suspect's disorientation by shining one of the flashlights directly into Straub's eyes.

"Relax, Georgie," Trooper Loomis said quietly. "No limbs high enough around here to string you up." Loomis had a dozen years in law enforcement, and knew the value of a rattled and nervous suspect. It was more difficult for them to concoct lies and fabricate stories if they were worried about other, more pressing concerns.

"We're just going for a ride," Collins added, helping

Straub step onto the rear bumper and up into the bed of the truck.

Deputy Blake popped the clutch and bolted away from the jail, jostling the riders in the bed of the pickup. After a few turns, Loomis shoved Straub to the wooden floorboards for his own protection against Blake's erratic driving. It wouldn't be a fun time if Loomis needed to explain to his superior, Inspector Treece, why a suspect had his skull cracked open like an egg after being thrown from a moving vehicle.

Inside the cab of the truck, Blake leaned forward so that his face was close to the windscreen and he could see into the darkness. Collins had told him to switch off the headlights after leaving the jail.

"When you get near the funeral home," Collins continued his instructions, "circle around the block a couple times. I want this guy on edge before we take him inside."

"Looks like he's ripe to crack," Blake observed.

It was almost 3:30 in the morning when the pickup came to an abrupt halt at the rear delivery entrance of the Gildersleeve funeral home. Straub was manhandled out of the bed of the truck towards the big barn door. Undersheriff Kutt pounded on the door with his fist.

Straub's eyes darted nervously from one officer to another, wringing his crippled hand with his good one.

After a moment, there was the sound of the bolts on the other side of the door being thrown. The noise seemed to echo down the vacant alley, causing a racoon to skitter away from a trash bin, its eyes reflecting silver in the light escaping the doorway.

"Highly irregular," the man who had opened the door commented to Kutt, expressing his displeasure. Preston Willows was an assistant undertaker who had had a long talk with Kutt earlier in the evening. His cooperation wasn't so much requested as demanded. His black suit, hair slicked back from his forehead and widow's peak with pomade, and sallow features seemed to Kutt like the required uniform of undertakers across the country. "The brother isn't going to approve, nor Reverend Griffith, I'm most certain."

"Show us the way, Mr. Willows," Kutt said, cutting short any further objections. Single-file, they headed towards the morgue of the funeral home, Willows followed by Kutt and Mulbar with Loomis, Collins and Blake following behind Straub. The hardwood floors creaked in the dark as they headed towards another door with a frosted glass window through which a light shone. Willows held the door as the procession filed into the morgue and remained outside the room, not wishing to bear witness to what the officers had in mind.

A lantern was perched at the head of a metal table, illuminating a shape draped in a white sheet. From the various contours and bumps, it was obviously the body of a woman.

"Georgie," Loomis said, pushing Straub nearer to the table with a hand in the middle of his back, "say hello again to Ms. Mallett."

From the far side of the table, Collins pulled the sheet off quickly, like Houdini performing some trick or a waiter artfully removing a tablecloth while leaving the china and crystal undisturbed. The motion revealed the naked and sutured body of Alice Mallett.

Straub tried to jump back, as if struck, but was held in place by Loomis.

"Why'd you take an ax to this fine woman, Georgie?" Loomis asked, his voice growing louder with every word.

"Never seen her," Straub protested.

"Why'd you kill her?" Collins inquired from his side

of the body.

"I didn't kill that lady."

"Sure you did, Georgie," Loomis now whispered into the suspect's ear. "Hacked her up, slit her throat, tore off her clothes."

"No, no," Straub cried. "I didn't kill her. I didn't kill nobody!"

"You'd like to touch her, wouldn't you, Georgie?"

"No."

"Sure you would, Georgie," Loomis now said louder, grabbing Straub's good hand at the wrist with both of his. "You want to touch her like that thirteen year-old you assaulted in Osceola County. Touch her like you did after slicing her throat wide open like a pig at a summer roast." His hand was forced closer to the cold, alabaster skin.

"Touch her, Mr. Straub," Collins said.

"No, no!" It took both Loomis and Officer Mulbar

to press Straub's hand to Alice Mallett's arm. Straub's eyes darted away from his hand, and looked wildly upon Mallett's lifeless face. His fingers recoiled as best they could, attempting to mutiny against his involuntarily directed hand.

"Get him in the truck," Collins said, tossing the white sheet back over the body, causing the lantern to flicker in the dark.

*****

Robert Brockie hushed his wife who nervously fussed behind him as he stood crouched at the front window of their parlor on the first floor, looking out towards the corner of Lansing Avenue and Jefferson. When he'd heard the commotion of a vehicle and boots hitting the pavement in front of his house, Brockie had looked over at the Gilbert alarm clock to read the luminous radium-coated hands to determine the time. He had to be up for his job at Crandall

Electric in just a couple hours, so his mood was initially sour

when he was awoken. At least it wasn't his neighbor's

damn rooster. Already on edge from the Mallett murder,

Brockie woke his wife and went down the stairs, a shotgun

in his hands.

"What can you see?" Elizabeth Brockie asked, for

the third time. Robert Brockie was now questioning why he

had nudged her awake.

"Please, Beth, pipe-down," he said, controlling his

tone. On top of everything else, he didn't need a shouting

match with his wife at four in the morning. "Looks like

some police in a pickup truck. Guess they all are looking for

more clues," he concluded, turning from the window,

cracking the chamber of the shotgun to remove the two

shells. With a household of boys, a loaded shotgun was just

trouble waiting to happen.

"Returning to the scene of the crime," Collins

announced to Straub outside in the yard. "Isn't that what they call it in those *Sherlock Holmes* books?"

"Ain't never been around here," Straub was already protesting. Kutt gave him a firm slap to the back of his head, sending Straub into the dirt of the garden.

"Nobody asked you a God damned question, Georgie." Kutt did not have any patience when a suspect got flippant. He yanked Straub up by the filthy collar of his inmate shirt and marched him around the property. Each spot was accompanied with a question, and then Straub's denials.

"You sneak up behind her?" Kutt asked at the location of where the initial blows were believed to have been delivered to Alice Mallett's head.

"No."

"Oh, so you just ran right up on her and brought down the ax?"

"No."

"You go through her groceries?" The spot where the eggs and flowers had be found.

"No."

"So you're a murderer, but not a thief?" Collins asked from the dark, again directing the beam of the flashlight into Straub's eyes.

"Why'd you move her body?" Loomis this time speaking up, his feet straddling the furrows in the tilled garden earth showing where the body had been dragged.

"He wanted to finish her off away from the house," Collins said, the officers having a conversation as if Straub wasn't even present.

"Big branches on that tree," Kutt offered. "Could riffle through her things, tear off her clothes, without prying eyes."

"Finishes her off with a blade," Loomis said. "Blood

had to have been everywhere, you hit both geysers in the neck. Must have bled like a stuck pig hanging from a slaughterhouse rafter," he speculated, again making a porcine comparison. "Rough work, huh, Georgie?"

"Wasn't here," Straub muttered, but seemingly with less conviction. He was wearing down, buffeted by questions from all around him in the dark night.

"We all know your type," Loomis said. "Doug Abbot knows your type, and knows you, in fact." Straub looked up upon mention of the name. When Loomis had been recruited to participate in the questioning of this suspect, he asked around in the small Jackson law enforcement community, followed-up on the information Collins already had about Straub's previous run-ins with the law.

"Doug Abbot who runs the show up at the State Pen here in Jackson?" Collins played along, Loomis having shared his information hours earlier.

"One in the same," Loomis answered. "Used to be a patrolman, picked up Georgie here after he did his stint for raping that little girl. Abbot told me that Georgie was getting back to his old ways while living with his mother on Blackstone near West North Street in the spring of 1913. Jumping out of the bushes, assaulting women. Judge Dahlem gave him a couple months at the House of Corrections in Detroit. Your own momma didn't know what to do with you, Georgie, so she had no argument with the judge sticking you in the pokey for a bit."

"That's none of your damn business."

"Before that, after going to the state pen for assaulting that girl, your family couldn't face the neighbors there in Hersey, could they? Had to pack up and move to Evart, right? In fact, everybody in Hersey knew better than to let their women near that George Straub."

"Your old man died, after you went in to do your six year stretch as a guest of the state. So your brother Claude brought your mother here to Jackson, huh?" Collins said.

"Then you lived with them after getting out," Loomis continued. "Even tried making a go at it back in Evart, but your kind wasn't welcome. You're a genuine black sheep of the family, ain't you, Georgie? Then you came back to Jackson. All you gave your momma was grief in her last years, didn't you?"

"Don't go bringing my mother into this," Straub muttered. "Ain't got nothing to do with none of this murdered woman nonsense you all have been talking. Now I want to get me some sleep. You all arrested me, I get my cot and my meals at the jail."

"Back to the ranch, gentlemen," Collins announced after shining a light on his wristwatch. "Next shift wants a talk with Mr. Straub."

*****

The next shift consisted of the Jackson City Police Department's chemist, Peter Keyzer, Deputy Sheriff Paul Julian, and the Jackson County Prosecutor, Michael Grove Hatch. Deputy Blake and Undersheriff Kutt were asked to sit in on the questioning, since they had observed Straub since they had taken him from the jail that morning. The other men had gone home to get some sleep, believing that they would be back at questioning the suspect by that afternoon, none of them thinking that the defiant Straub would confess any time soon, if at all.

Trooper Harold Mulbar was tasked, before his head hit any pillows, to stop by the residences of Inspector Arthur Treece and Detective Juan Piper. It was believed that they had returned from Ohio, and having had led the primary investigation from the beginning, ought to be involved in the questioning of George Straub. However, after checking in at the State Police post, Mulbar received information regarding

Little Bear Smith being seen drinking in a saloon due north

in Mason. In the excitement of the information, and

Treece's scolding still fresh in his memory, Mulbar grabbed

another officer, a department Dodge, and a shotgun and hit

the road to Mason, totally remiss in his duty to notify Piper

and Treece.

The questioning of Straub was continued in the

deserted cafeteria at the jail, one of the few spots large

enough to accommodate all of the men. They sat on long

benches at wooden tables, all of the furniture painted

institutional green. The administrators believed that the

color suppressed the appetite, and the county could therefore

save on the cost of feeding inmates.

"Did you know her?" Peter Keyzer began after

several moments of silence, placing a mug of black coffee

before Straub. An urn in the kitchen was kept full by a

civilian jail employee or inmate trusty for the guards around

the clock. Keyzer kept his voice low but animated, to keep

the suspect's attention but in a non-threatening manner.

Besides being the department's chemist, Keyzer's advanced

degrees and education made him an integral part of

interrogations in the rare case of this magnitude to hit

Jackson.

"Ever seen her around?" Keyzer said, attempting to

ease Straub into his story.

"Some folks have got it coming, George. Did she have it

coming?"

"Naw," Straub finally answered, taking a moment to

blow over the rim of the coffee mug and taking a tentative

sip. "I didn't know her."

It was the chink in Straub's armor of denial, that first

leak in the dam before it all comes rushing out. Prosecutor

Hatch began scribbling in his notebook. Deputies Julian and

Blake sat silently away from the table, not wanting to queer the moment, almost holding their breath.

"What were you doing Thursday night, before you killed her?" Keyzer delicately continued, stepping cautiously onto thin ice.

"Went to pay off a debt on Cooper Street," Straub said, not denying that second half of Keyzer's question. "I got my place on Seymour Avenue, but sometimes I stay where the cooking's good. The Fowlers rent out a room to me for a couple weeks at a time when I'm flush. Mrs. Fowler makes a roast on Sundays, worth the week's cost of board alone. I made even with them Thursday then kept on walking down Cooper."

"Were you out of money then?"

"Pretty much, just a few nickels jingling in my pocket," Straub answered. "Might as well have empty pockets if you can't scratch together at least a dollar. My road construction job don't pay until Thursday."

"So you figured you'd rob somebody, huh? Easy money, that's understandable." Keyzer's ability to express empathy for suspects like Straub was what made him successful. The suspect didn't feel judged, but felt obliged to explain to a reasonable fellow like Keyzer.

"Been trying off and on to do just that," Straub said. "Tried getting some change from some women folk, jump out and spook them, get some money."

"You'd tried that earlier on South Elm?" Keyzer asked, referring to the assault on Martha Quick which Timmons and Piper had been investigating around the time of the murder.

"Yes, sir, but I picked a feisty one," he recalled. "Even though I had me a knife, she started making a fuss, so I had to run off."

"Had to come up with a way to make it work, huh,

George?"

"Sure," he answered. "So I'm heading down Cooper towards Lansing, figure I got to get me a weapon, something more powerful than my knife."

"Something like an ax?" Keyzer volunteered.

"Yes, sir, done found me an ax behind back of a house on Lansing, I think. Went on down and found a quiet spot near Jefferson. Not even all the traffic from the circus seemed to come past, so I hid in the bushes."

Hatch wrote, "laying in wait" down in his notebook, already planning charges for the county's grand jury.

"Then you spotted your mark?"

"Yes, sir," Straub answered, casually rubbing his gimp hand. "Lady coming down the street with a bag of groceries, umbrella. Figured she'd have some money on her, at least change from the store. She got close, and I came out after she passed. Tried to sneak up on her, but I tripped coming out of the bushes."

"She see you?" Keyzer asked, imagining Alice Mallett's horror. "She get spooked?"

"And how," Straub said, as if proud of an accomplishment. "Dropped her bag and tried to run on off down Lansing towards Jefferson. I caught up and took a swing or two, can't remember exactly, and down she went to the ground."

"You hit her again?"

"You're darn tooting, mister," Straub said, becoming more animated. "She hit the ground and I was starting to shove my kerchief into her mouth when I seen she wasn't out. She started fighting, screeching like a train's brakes, so I turned the ax around and clubbed her in the head." From his discussions with Coroner Mills, Keyzer knew this to have been the blow which crushed Alice Mallett's skull.

"Then you moved her?" Kutt asked, breaking the

flow of the conversation.

"No," Straub said, shooting a scowl in Kutt's direction.

"Did you move her, George?" Keyzer repeated the question.

"I dragged her nearer the street," Straub answered as if Kutt had never even spoken. "Figured that if somebody was home in the house, I was too close. I took her through a garden to a big oak closer to Jefferson."

"Was she unconscious at this point?"

"You mean asleep? Yeah, she was asleep."

"And that's when you took some liberties with her body, right, George? She was a little older, but still a Sheba. Might as well come clean on all of it," Keyzer added, noting some hesitation.

"Sure, she was spiffy," Straub conceded. "I tore open her dress, looking for money and the like."

"Assault of a sexual nature then took place," was Hatch's interpretation which he wrote down in his notes. Hatch was not the type of prosecutor to give any benefit of the doubt to a suspect in a murder case.

"Go through her purse?"

"No, figured I ought to be getting out of there after the commotion that lady caused, screaming and carrying on so." The denial of going through Mallett's purse only strengthened Hatch's future argument that Straub's tearing of her clothing was for perverse sexual thrill and gratification. More rope.

"Remember me asking you about being drunk the other night?" Keyzer asked. "Before Detective Collins asked you some questions?"

"Sure."

"Were you drinking the night you killed this woman?"

"Drinking? Sure."

"Were you drunk?"

"No."

"No mitigation of being intoxicated," Hatch scribbled with a slight grin.

"Then what, George?"

"Finished the job. Took the ax to her neck. She had to have been dying, anyway, so what's the difference?" Straub's answer exhibited the callousness Hatch treasured in a defendant. Those words would be the rope he would use to figuratively hang Straub at trial.

This was one point which differed from Dr. Seybold's conclusions at the autopsy. The nearly severing of Alice Mallett's head from her neck had not been caused by a hunting knife, but rather, by the ax. It must have been an extremely sharp ax, Keyzer thought, or Straub was lying about using the ax to finish her off. That was something

Keyzer had seen in many of the criminals he had had the occasion to interview over the years. Sometimes they wouldn't deny committing the deed, but denied the manner and means of its commission. He did not always understand fellows like this George Straub, and he slept better at night for it.

"Lots of blood, George?"

"Of course, lots," he said, almost pleased with himself like a child accomplishing a task, or a cat delivering a mouse to its owner's door mat. His pride was hideous and repulsive, but his interrogator withheld his personal feelings. "Had to dump some of my clothes on the way home," Straub continued.

"In the Drexel addition?" Keyzer asked, referring to a section of town where articles of men's clothing had been reportedly found after the murder.

"Probably around there."

"Mr. Straub," Prosecutor Hatch now spoke, his technique more in line with that of Keyzer than Vern Kutt. Bees with honey, he thought. "I'm Prosecutor Hatch."

"I know, Mr. Hatch," Straub said. "I'd have voted for you if I hadn't done time in the pen. Six years in Jackson."

"I appreciate that, Mr. Straub," Hatch said, not knowing how else to respond. "Mr. Straub, if we took you back to the area of Lansing near Jefferson, would you mind walking us through what you just told Mr. Keyzer?"

"Long as that sumbitch ain't standing next to me," he said, pointing at Kutt.

"No good bastard," Kutt began, stepping forward. Julian and Blake had the presence of mind to block Kutt's path.

"Fair enough," Hatch said quickly, pointing towards the door and giving Kutt a stern look. The water was flowing over the dam, and Hatch didn't want Kutt acting like the little Dutch boy, causing Straub to cease his cooperation. Red in the face, but acknowledging the situation, Kutt walked out of the cafeteria.

"Let us get some vehicles ready and then we'll be off," Keyzer said. With Deputies Julian and Blake standing guard in the cafeteria, the others stepped out behind Kutt.

"Get Inspector Treece and Detectives Piper and Timmons down here," Hatch instructed Keyzer. "Didn't someone get sent to fetch them?"

"Yes, but I'll do the same."

"Good, Pete," Hatch said. "And you might as well get somebody down here from the *Cit-Pat*. If we give them the scoop, they ought to cooperate and not publish the details until after we've substantiated Straub's version of events. Booth and his folks at the paper are on board, so that shouldn't be a problem. Been enough false suspects already," he commented, having been kept abreast of the other individuals upon which the investigators had previously focused.

"I think you all are being a might bit too charitable to him," Kutt voiced his objection. "Giving that fool coffee and such."

"Take it easy, Vern," Hatch said, who had known the undersheriff since high school. "If he attempts to flee or otherwise break detention, I won't lose any sleep if you gun-down the bastard."

CHAPTER EIGHT

Tuesday Evening, June 13, 1922

The original investigators on the Alice Mallett murder case had been located, awoken, and rushed to the Brockie property. Treece was steamed at Trooper Mulbar not having gotten him and Piper prior to Straub's confession, but his anger diminished a bit when he was informed that Mulbar and another trooper had successfully apprehended their fugitive. Little Bear Smith had been found passed-out in a roadhouse outside Mason, Michigan. Mulbar and his partner couldn't fit their handcuffs around Smith's massive wrists, so they hog-tied the unconscious Indian and stuffed him in the back of the Dodge for the ride back to Jackson.

At Robert Brockie's house that afternoon, George Straub led investigators through the garden and again across the lawn to the big oak near the street, this time narrating

like a tour guide. Inspector Treece walked beside Straub,

Timmons and Piper observing from behind. Since they did

not wish to drawn any undue attention to the scene, they

replaced the striped county inmate shirt Straub had been

wearing with a gray workshirt, and permitted him to walk

around without handcuffs or shackles. Treece and the

detectives, as befitting their positions with their agencies,

wore suits instead of uniforms, so Straub did not stand out

from the group when observed from a distance. An eager

Vern Kutt, who was in uniform, patrolled along the side of

the Brockie residence, shotgun in hand, almost hoping that

Straub would make a break for it. A newspaper reporter, the

same Gitanes-smoking reporter who had traveled with

Timmons, was invited to come along. The publisher and

editor-in-chief again agreed to not print details of Straub's

confession until his account was substantiated as best it

could.

Despite their intention not to garner the attention of any citizens, they were spotted by a man and woman walking down the street together. Piper looked over as they strolled down the sidewalk, and grew interested when the woman stopped in her tracks and grabbed the man's arm, then timidly pointed in the direction of Straub. Piper walked over to the couple.

"Something wrong, ma'am," Piper asked, showing his detective's shield.

"That man, the one in the gray shirt," she said. "My husband and I saw him last Thursday night around here. We live just around the block on Adams Street."

"We don't think he lives around here," the husband added. "He was loitering in the grass over there, near the bushes. We were on our way home from the circus."

"Did you see him doing anything else?" Piper asked.

"Besides looking like a drugstore cowboy hanging around?" the woman asked.

"I'd have told him to scram, but I had my wife with me. We know that's Bob Brockie's place, and he'd be sure to run that drunk off his property when he saw him."

"Need to ask you nice folks to head on down to the police station, ask for Captain Fagan. Tell him I sent you down to give a statement, tell him what you just told me. Tell him you saw 'our guy' around here last Thursday night. Can you do that?" Piper asked.

"Sure, 'our guy,'" the man repeated. "This got something to do with that murder, right? The matron from the Crittendon Home, right?"

"Yup, but let's keep this to ourselves, okay? We're still investigating. Don't tell anyone else except for Captain Jack Fagan."

"Absolutely, sir," the woman said, pulling her

husband by the arm to get away from the glare of George

Straub.

After describing his flight from the scene, Straub

walked the investigators down the street to the nearby yard

from which he had acquired the ax. As they were reviewing

additional details with Straub, Timmons called to the City of

Jackson Police Department and requested that Peter Keyzer

bring the suspected murder weapon to their location. Once

there, and after Straub acknowledged that it was the

instrumentality of death he had used on Alice Mallett,

Timmons rapped on the front door of the residence, the ax

still wrapped in butcher's paper. Predictably, the owner had

not even been aware of the absence of his property. Like

many of the homes in town, the kitchen stove and a potbelly

in the parlor helped to provide heat in the cold winter

months. This being June, the owner had not touched the ax

since he had sharpened it several weeks before after clearing stumps to put in a driveway to his new garage.

Straub was taken back to the jail without incident, and without giving Undersheriff Vern Kutt any excuse to discharge his shotgun.

Peter Keyzer, Sean Timmons, and Donald Phelps, another Jackson City Police detective, went to the Fowler residence. There, Mrs. Fowler corroborated Straub's story of stopping by Thursday evening or night to settle his outstanding debt. From the pungent burning smells emanating from Mrs. Fowler's kitchen, Keyzer couldn't figure what was so good about her cooking. Her hair was up in a bun, her apron soiled with grease and dusted with buckwheat flour. She noted, that despite Straub's protests, he had been drinking that night.

"Moonshine," Mrs. Fowler said. "That's what I figured he was drinking, the way his breath made my eyes water. I took what he owed us, and sent him on his way."

"Anything else?" Phelps asked.

"George is a strange man," she observed. "He's been in trouble in the past, from what I understand, but I ain't never had any trouble with him. He was working, paying up what he owed folks. Besides," she added, "he just loves my cooking. Figure I ought to think about opening a restaurant, give the Central Café some competition."

"Good luck with that," Keyzer said, ending the conversation on that note.

*****

Art Treece and Juan Piper delivered the news of the solving of Alice Mallett's murder to her brother Harold at the home of Dr. Grace Hendricks on West Cortland where Harold Mallett was staying. Requests by Mallett to view the man who had murdered his sister were declined, Mallett's agitated state giving the officers concern that he would attempt to do harm to their suspect. When Mallett pushed the subject, Treece was required to put him in his place.

"Mr. Mallett," Treece began, calm but forceful. "If I was in your shoes, I'd want nothing better than to have some time alone with this fellow. And given the chance, only one of us would walk out of that room. Now, while I can understand your feelings, I can't allow a situation to occur where you even have the opportunity to get yourself in such a pickle. It just won't do to have that happen, not on my watch."

"I want justice for my sister," Mallett said. "She deserves it, and I demand it."

"Don't you worry, Mr. Mallett," Piper interjected. "Y'all will get your justice

The final home edition of *The Jackson Citizen Patriot* began to hit the stands at Ellsworth Pharmacy and Davison's Drug Store on Granson about the time the investigators were leaving the distraught Harold Mallett.

Discussion of the gory facts contained in the article was dominant among the men getting haircuts and shaves at Howard's Barber Shop, and the ladies and gentlemen among the first round of diners at the Central Café . Lessons at the Barnard Music Company on South Mechanic Street across from the Majestic Theatre were cancelled so that Mr. Barnard could close up the store and attend an emergency meeting of the city council.

Additional pieces of information flowed into the police station as readers viewed the details in the newspaper which accompanied a photograph of George Straub. Residents from the Crittendon Home, escorted by Alice Mallett's former superior Ada Smith, came in to recount encounters with Straub. He'd been seen at various times lurking around that property, leering at the young widowed and unwed mothers. Some discussed how Straub had attempted to break in to homes around that part of Jackson.

"I've always said we need more services at the Home," Ada Smith said, taking the opportunity to repeat a familiar chorus. "More street lights, take down some of those overgrown trees along the street. Wouldn't hurt to have a patrolman take a keener interest in his beat."

*****

"Looks like we might have ourselves some trouble outside," Coroner Mills stated, looking out the second floor window of an office in the jail. About nine o'clock in the evening, he and Prosecutor Hatch had been meeting at the jail to prepare the presentation for the grand jury. Hatch wanted all of the medical details straight in his head, and had been in the process of discussing some inconsistencies in Straub's confession and the autopsy findings. His hair was disheveled, working in shirtsleeves rolled up to his elbows. It had been a long day, and the end was not yet in sight.

Upon hearing the coroner's words, Hatch got up from the table and looked out the window for himself. In the light from the street lamps, he could make out many dozen, if not a couple hundred, figures making their way down the street towards the front steps of the jail.

"Got the feeling that's a God damned lynch mob," Hatch said. "Doubt Jackson's seen one of those since the turn of the century."

"Well, the leader of the pack appears to be the same Harold Mallett I was introduced to this afternoon at Gildersleeve's."

"Who's downstairs watching our popular prisoner?" Hatch asked.

"Deputy Julian, Vern Kutt, and that state guy Mulbar, the one that brought in that Indian," Mills answered. "Think we can keep them out?"

"Not a chance," Hatch said, "not if they want in.

Too many angry folks out there, from the looks of it. Don't suppose they'd listen if I reminded them that vengeance belongs to the Lord, do you?"

"They look mighty crazed. They may start calling out for Barabbas, for all I know. And I do see more than one length of rope in some hands out there."

"Christ," Hatch said, not one to frequently use the name in vain. "Let's get downstairs and figure this out." They rushed down to the cell block in which Straub was being held. He was the only individual in custody at the jail that night, the other prisoners having been moved to a wing of the Michigan State Prison in the afternoon, including Little Bear Smith.

"Seen that crowd?" Kutt asked. He had run home for a meal with his family, and caught sight of it upon his return. "Told those fools to go on home, but they ain't listening."

"They seem to mean to cause harm?" Hatch asked.

"Can't tell. Harold Mallett seems to be leading the group. Lot of ladies in the crowd, so I can't see them getting too rough."

"One never can tell," Hatch said. "Get calls out to the fire chief, and might as well ring up the State Police H.Q. in Lansing, have them send down some bodies. Art Treece's boys have been worn so thin from the Jackson post, I don't know how much help they'd be. Let's get some city officers over here, too."

"What about the prisoner?" Mulbar asked.

"I've got an idea, gentlemen," Mills said. "I'll call the fire chief, somebody else give Lansing a call."

"Probably ought to get him out of here," Kutt suggested.

"I don't know if you're genuinely concerned for his safety," Hatch said, "or you just want another chance to see if he'll make a break for it."

By ten, the crowd was estimated at two hundred people or more, including women and children. Food vendors had set up on the fringes of the mob, giving the appearance and producing the atmosphere of a carnival.

Several officers from the police department, as well as available sheriff's deputies, mingled through the crowd, attempting to keep the lid on the simmering situation. Obvious rabble-rousers attempting to further agitate the crowd were encouraged to be on their way, leading to a few minor skirmishes.

Harold Mallett stood at the center of the largest portion of the mob, literally standing on a wooden soapbox so that all could see and hear him.

"Justice for my sister," he was saying, "won't be denied. They've got the murderous, son of a bitch in that there jail, waiting for his day in court. Alice didn't get any opportunity to be heard. She just got an ax in the head for all of her good work in this city."

"We ought to go and get him," a man in the crowd shouted.

"Absolutely," Mallett responded.

"He's gonna get them whipped up," Fire Chief Paul King said to Prosecutor Hatch. They stood on the front steps of the jail about one hundred feet from the group, surveying the mob. "I got my men at the station ready to bring out the hoses if necessary."

"This could turn into a real mess," Hatch said, watching a woman approach, breaking out of the crowd and past a phalanx of city officers and accompanied by a broad-shouldered man. She was short, a feature accentuated by a long dress which followed on the street behind her like the train of a wedding gown. A Bible with a new white plastic cover was held firmly in her hands. It was her third attempt to enter.

"You ought to turn that fiend over to us," she said to Hatch.

"You are really trying my patience, ma'am," Hatch said slowly. "That you, Ms. Ryan?" he then asked, identifying Helen Ryan. "The only way you are going to catch a glance of this fellow is in a court of law."

"And if it ain't Sailor Lewis," Chief King said, looking at Ms. Ryan's escort. The big man was a local boxer from days past, still recognizable for his size and nose flattened from too many jabs. King reached out and shook the semi-famous fighter's hand. "Tough luck on your last fight. Losing by decision must be worse than by knock-out."

"I'm sure the judge's were paid-off," Lewis said, apparently forgetting the task at hand. Hatch was impressed with the fire chief's smooth skills of distraction.

"Please, people," another raised voice called out from the crowd. It was Reverend Parrott from St. Paul's Episcopal, trying to hold sway over the mob, taking his turn on the upended soap box. "Go on home, let the authorities do their job. You all must trust in the Lord, and trust in the authorities."

"You go home, Reverend," a man responded. There was an uproar and laughter when Parrott was pelted with a volley of raw eggs. Stained yellow and white from yolks and shells, Parrott retreated back through the crowd, satisfied that he had done his duty.

"You brought that stuff for Mills, right?" Hatch asked Chief King after Ryan and Lewis had disappeared back into the crowd.

"Sure did," he said. "Ain't that the coroner's Marmon pulling out of the alley?"

The Marmon Model 34 automobile's body was the

color of faded yellow, the black top up. The driver revved

the six cylinder engine to clear a path. Trooper Mulbar

stood on the driver's side running board. Barely visible in

the back seat was a figure dressed in a blue wool uniform

with Jackson City Fire Department insignia on the shoulders

and lapels. Deputy Julia sat beside him. The crowd parted

for the automobile, and then closed back in as it took off

down Jackson. The people moved closer towards the front

entrance of the jail.

More time passed with more shoving and shouts for

riot. The street lamps began to glow as the sun had set and

the waning moon started to come up.

"Here comes more state troopers in a Black Maria,"

Chief King said, noting a state paddywagon which parked

near the food vendors.

"Clear out, Hatch," a voice called out from the

crowd. "Give us this bastard."

"We've got a rope," another announced.

A considerable portion of the mob moved forward menacingly, like a wave crashing on the breakers in Lake Erie. A barrier of city police and state troopers, led by Captain Jack Fagan, rebuffed the first rush of about fifty men, violence limited to pushing and a few jabs.

"Signal the troopers," Hatch said to a police officer who had joined them on the front steps of the jail. He sensed that things were about to blow. The officer took off his uniform cap and waved it above his head.

Several troopers exited the police wagon, tying handkerchiefs over their faces like railroad bandits of the past. Sergeant Alfred Bolan, a hardened veteran from the War, was identifiably leading that group of trooper, eschewing any mask for himself. He'd eaten worse things than CN gas in France. They ran away from the crowd, towards the fire escape ladders on surrounding buildings.

The men quickly mounted the ladders, carrying olive drab satchels slung over their shoulders by leather straps. The people were so focused on the front of the jail, they did not appear to notice the tactical deployment of troopers.

Before the crowd could react, the troopers began to lob chloroacetophenone bombs into their midst from the rooftops of the surrounding buildings. The tear gas bombs popped loudly before emitting blinding, choking gas. Many of the individuals, mostly those who had joined the mob for some social aspect, dispersed immediately, coughing with their eyes streaming tears down their cheeks. Women sheltered their children as best they could in the folds of their dresses and they fled into the alleys and cross streets around the jail on North Jackson near Main.

Sergeant Bolan descended from his rooftop position, only to be carried off in a crush of fleeing people towards the rear of the jail.

"Gassing women and children," one of the men shouted at Bolan, seeing the satchel still hanging from his shoulder.

"All to protect some murderer," another called out as a circle of crying and coughing angry men began to close in on the lone officer. One of the men brandished a length of pipe.

"Another step," Bolan said, drawing his service revolver from the holster on his right hip, "and I'll plug your guts with lead. There might be more than six of you, but who'll be the lucky six I send to the morgue." The pipe dropped to the gravel alley with a thud as the group immediately dispersed. They'd have to seek satisfaction elsewhere.

Affected by the tear gas as well, Hatch and Fire Chief King retreated into the jail, going up the stairs to the protection of the administrative offices. Just behind them, a more determined group of rioters, led by the Bible-carrying Helen Ryan and the boxer Lewis, rushed through the front doors, toppling a few uniformed officers. Harold Mallett brought up the rear.

With clouds of tear gas following the group of bodies into the jail entrance, the mob continued hacking from their exposure as they progressed to the cell blocks on the lower levels. Through their watery, red-rimmed eyes, those who had invaded the jail found their search to be unfruitful. No George Straub was to be found anywhere, nor any inmates for that matter.

Sailor Lewis emerged from the front entrance, his physical and social stature hushing the crowd. By his side was Harold Mallett.

"Where's Straub?"

"Bring him out."

The question and command was repeated by several

in the remaining mob outside on North Jackson.

"Ain't in the jail," Lewis said in response.

"It's true," Mallett concurred. "Place is empty. They must have smuggled him out by automobile."

"To hell with this group," Mrs. Ryan called when she took a position on the top step in front of the county jail. "You men let him get away. It'll be up to the women folk to see justice done for Alice Mallett. We don't get him tonight, we'll get him at arraignment."

Just then, the coroner's Marmon came careening around the corner from Main Street, Trooper Mulbar at the wheel, driving in his usual reckless manner.

"There," Ryan called, "there's the car that must have whisked the murderer away."

Mulbar slammed on the brakes, fish-tailing to a stop before swinging the big automobile around and racing away south on Jackson. Half a dozen men raced to nearby vehicles to go after the trooper, who was unbeknownst to them acting as a decoy.

"The rest of you with autos, let's split up," Sailor Lewis shouted. "We'll check all the county seats around here and find where they've hidden the murderer."

"What you're going to do is go home and cool your heads," Sergeant Bolan announced, coming from around the side of the jail, revolver in one hand, CN bomb in the other, surrounded by a considerable contingent of regrouped officers. "Or we'll split them for you, and then stick you in this here empty jail. Party's over, and we won't have any more vigilante talk."

With the renewed show of force, even the most ardent rioter put on his hat and headed home. Fire Chief King and Prosecutor Hatch were collected from the jail offices by Captain Fagan and his men.

Hatch put on his coat and hat and headed home for a

few hours, the county's taxpayers having gotten more than

an honest day's work out of their top law enforcer.

CHAPTER NINE

Wednesday, June 14, 1922

The streets around the Jackson County Jail

downtown were being swept clean by city sanitation workers

in the morning. The debris included newspapers, food

wrappers, and spent tear gas bomb canisters. Straub was

being held at the Lansing city jail. The previous night, he

had first been driven away from the jail in the coroner's

private automobile, and then transferred to a state vehicle

which took him to Lansing, arriving around midnight. The

other county prisoners had since been returned from the state

prison back to the county facility.

City Manager Thomas Crary held a conference along

with Prosecutor Hatch, Inspector Treece, and Police Chief

Bean at the same jailhouse steps where the unrest had

occurred. Crary praised the city police, county sheriff's

department, and the State Police representatives who had quelled the mob from the previous night.

"No lynch mobs in our fair city," Crary said. "There haven't been in years, and we are not going to go back to those days. Our fine law enforcement officers made sure of that last night, and will continue to do so in a dignified and professional manner." There was no mention of using tear gas on women and children, nor the fact that the jail had been abdicated for a short period of time to the rabble.

"Rest assured," Crary continued to the audience, "with the apprehension of the fiend George Straub, and the excellent performance of the authorities, the fine law-abiding citizens can enjoy safety and security here in the city of Jackson."

Straub spent Wednesday morning having a breakfast of eggs and country ham, courtesy of the Lansing taxpayers. For some inexplicable reason, the jailers permitted Straub to have copies of the *Lansing State Journal*. After reading

nearly a week's worth of Associated Press articles about the

Alice Mallett murder and investigation, Straub requested the

presence of Peter Keyzer and Jackson County Prosecutor M.

Grove Hatch. By early afternoon, the men were together

again, this time in Straub's cell.

"Got to tell you gentlemen, that I didn't do the deed,"

was how Straub began. "Was this Negro from that circus.

Meadowlark's his name." Before his skeptical audience,

Straub described that after leaving the Fowler residence, he

came upon this Meadowlark, who introduced himself.

Taking from Straub's appearance and disposition that he

was in need of money, Meadowlark asked Straub to join him

as an accomplice in robbery.

"Was the Negro," Straub claimed, "had an ax with

him. Told me where he got that ax, that's how I could show

you the woodpile it was at. Meadowlark took that ax to the

lady, ripped her clothes open, looked for money in her purse. I was just there, didn't know what he had planned until he just started swinging."

Keyzer asked a series of questions, but was unconvinced of Straub's recantation of his earlier confession, and the inclusion of Clark Meadowlark in the incident. Seeing the stack of newspapers only solidified Keyzer's belief that this second confession was pure fabrication to cast guilt upon the other man about whom Straub had obviously read.

"Quit giving him any more God damned newspapers," Hatch swore at the jailers after leaving Straub in his cell. "Give him the Good Book, he wants to read anything."

Keyzer and Hatch exited the jail and walked down the block, smoking cigarettes, to the corner of Michigan and Capitol Avenues, the domed Michigan State Capitol in view.

"Horseshit," Hatch said simply. "Too late for that damned fool to try to put this off on some other fellow. Didn't they clear this Meadowlark?"

"Pretty much," Keyzer said, who had become the clearinghouse of all the investigation's information. "They're still holding him. And we took plaster casts of the footprints in that garden, before everyone trampled the hell out of it. They match Straub's shoes."

"Well," Hatch said, pitching his cigarette butt into the street, "wire Jackson and have them bring up Meadowlark. Art Treece ought to come up, too. We'll talk to him again up here."

"News is probably out about where we brought Straub," Keyzer said, voicing what was also on Hatch's mind.

"The Ingham County Prosecutor is a friend of mine," Hatch said. "He'll scratch up a good hiding place for Straub and Meadowlark while we figure this out."

"We get in another bind like at the jail," Keyzer said, "Vandercook's liable to call in the Calvary."

"Don't want to see any Michiganders get their heads split open on account of pile of trash like that Straub," Hatch responded. "But for the better angels of my nature, I might leave the keys to his cell out front of that there capitol building. Invite the public to do my job."

CHAPTER TEN

Thursday, June 15, 1922

From the newspaper articles concerning Straub's dubious second confession attempting to implicate Clark Meadowlark, participants from Tuesday night's vigilante mob, including Harold Mallett, learned of the murderer's location. On Wednesday, newspaper reporters and photographers had even been permitted to view Straub, as if a sideshow attraction, as the authorities believed it acceptable to reveal Straub's current location.

Just after midnight, Thursday morning, Mallett led about fifty men north to Lansing in a caravan of automobiles and pickup trucks, their pace quickened by rage, and for some, by hooch. Another contingent was simultaneously proceeding to the Ingham county seat in Mason, to check that jail in case Straub had been sent there instead.

"What's this?" Mallett said from the passenger side seat of the Model T in which he was riding. The caravan came to an abrupt halt outside the Lansing city limits by a blinding barricade of automobile headlamps. Michigan State troopers, most armed with Thompson submachine guns, stepped in front of the lights, ordering the Jackson men from their vehicles. Their weapons were held at port arms, but fingers were laced through the trigger guards, ready for action.

"Listen here," one of the armed men said, a foot resting on the bumper of his Ford, Thompson pointed nonchalantly at the ground. It was Colonel Roy C. Vandercook himself, public safety commission for the State of Michigan, and leader of the Michigan State Police. His physical appearance was as impressive as his reputation. Several of the men from Jackson recognized him, and quickly informed Mallett of that fact.

"This here is my city, my capital, and as far as you all should be concerned, my state," Vandercook stated with undisputed authority. "I understand you all caused a bit of disturbance in Jackson the other night, gave the police and some of my troopers a difficult time." He glared at those around him.

"There will not be, gentlemen, an encore of that occurrence here in Lansing. You the brother?" he then asked, pointing the muzzle of his gun towards Harold Mallett.

"Yes, sir," he mumbled humbly.

"You are not going to get a chance to lynch or otherwise harm this Straub fellow. He is to be prosecuted in a court of law, properly. However, Mr. Mallett, if it will sate you some, you will be permitted to view this man."

"Thank you, sir," Mallett responded.

"So that we are clear, gentlemen," Vandercook

addressed the group as a whole, "you will be escorted to the city jail by my troopers. Once there, Chief Alfred Seymour will handle the viewing." The troopers climbed back into their vehicles, as did the civilians. Vandercook paused to shout back at those men.

"And just so you know that outbursts won't be tolerated," he warned, "my men have been ordered to shoot to kill if there is any trouble."

That stern warning seemed to have the desired effect. Harold Mallett, and a limited number of companions, were permitted to enter the Lansing jail and the cell block containing George Straub. Over two dozen state and local officers armed with Thompsons, riot guns, and tear gas oversaw the viewing, with Chief Seymour of the Lansing City Police Department leading the procession.

Through a small glass window in the main door of the cell block, Mallett and the others were able to view his sister's murderer. Straub appeared tired and dejected, if not down right bored with the matter, when he looked up to observe those observing him.

After the group from Jackson was escorted back out of the city limits, both Straub and Clark Meadowlark, who had arrived earlier with Inspector Treece, were secluded in the holding facilities at the headquarters of the Michigan State Police.

"Nice work getting this Straub," Colonel Vandercook was congratulating Treece. They were in Vandercook's office along with Prosecutor Hatch and Major Robert Marsh, Vandercook's first assistant and the deputy commissioner of the State Department of Public Safety. "You've done a fine job, Art. I figure you'll wind up a captain, if not major, by the time Hatch here gets the key thrown away on this Straub."

"Just don't be eyeing my job," Marsh joked.

"Thank you, sir," Treece said, slightly uncomfortable with the accolades. He had always considered himself just a cog in the system, going back to his Calvary days.

"What about this other man, Meadowlark? Straub's story about him being involved hold any water?"

"No, sir," Treece answered. "Straub's just trying to backtrack on his confession. He's had some time to sit around and think that he'd rather be out. He must remember his six years in Jackson being none too pleasant."

"Well, I trust you gentlemen to get this resolved. That Harold Mallett going to cause any more problems? He's mourning right now, but he doesn't want to be hurting."

"Don't think so, Roy," Hatch said. His stature placed him on a first name basis with Vandercook. "After he saw Straub, he told me that he isn't going to cause any more grief or difficulties. I think he's come around from his initial feelings, and now he's just thankful that Art and the rest got their man."

"Well, that's something," Vandercook commented, tugging the cuffs of his uniform. "Guess it would be a shame if the Michigan Central had to send two pine boxes out West for planting."

CHAPTER ELEVEN

Friday, June 16, 1922

It was one week after the heinous butchering of Ms. Alice Mallett on the city streets of Jackson, Michigan. In Lansing that morning, Jackson County Prosecutor Hatch appeared to have a final resolution to the investigation into the murder.

Investigators had again questioned Clark Meadowlark, most strenuously. Despite the belief that Straub was simply attempting to defray responsibility by insisting that Meadowlark had the lead role in the murder, the detectives used a jaundiced eye when listening to Meadowlark. After extensive questioning, they decided that he had had no involvement whatsoever. They were not, however, finished with Meadowlark.

"But you could help us out, anyway," Van Loomis

said.

"Shouldn't we have Treece or at least that Pete Keyzer here to assist?" Major Robert Marsh asked. At Colonel Vandercook's suggestion, Marsh had been recruited to assist Harry Collins and Van Loomis in the renewed questioning of George Straub.

"Frankly, sir," Collins said, "we've got some peculiar methods those two would be better off not witnessing. Colonel Vandercook and Hatch said that you'd go along with our plans."

"Well, let's get to it then," Marsh said, awaiting instructions.

Later, Straub was escorted from his cell to the laundry room of the Michigan State Police headquarters. Inmates serving local time at the Ingham County Jail worked in the laundry, washing sheets and pressing uniforms.

The laundry consisted of a large room in the

basement level of the building, brimming with steam pipes and machines. The air was hot and thick, even though the current shift was on break and the machinery was not in use. It was not a choice assignment for inmates. Like many technological advances since the turn of the century, automation and industrialization did not always mean an easier life for those who manned the machines. At times, newer developments, like these huge washing vats and steam pressed, just meant that men could be worked harder.

"Now what you doing?" Straub asked, looking first to Loomis, and then to Collins. Neither responded, instead nudging Straub on towards the back. They were all perspiring form the heat, but the sweat had started pouring down Straub's face as soon as he had been removed from his cell.

Near a large steam press, Major Marsh stood beside a low table. On top of the table a sheet-covered body was resting, reminiscent of the scene with Alice Mallett's body at the Gildersleeve funeral home.

"Can't show me that woman again," Straub protested. "Can't use that trick again. I done told you that the Negro did it."

"This Negro? Mr. Meadowlark?" Marsh asked, removing the sheet to exposed Clark Meadowlark. The man was still, his eyes closed as if dead, a hangman's noose secured taunt around his neck.

"Oh, God," Straub cried, holding his crippled hand to his mouth.

"This isn't Jackson, Mr. Straub," Major Marsh said. "We do thing differently here in the state capital." Marsh tossed the sheet back over the body and Straub was hustled back to the entrance of the laundry, out of sight of Meadowlark.

"You implicated that man, and justice was served,"

Loomis said. "Don't think you ain't gonna pay the piper, too, Georgie."

"I did it alone," Straub cried. "I came at her with the ax and struck her down. I don't know who that Negro was on that there table. I just read about him in the papers. I figured I'd only get it half as bad if you all thought there was two of us involved."

"That sure is some odd logic," Collins said. "So you're saying that you did this all alone? That you killed Alice Mallett last Thursday night, with an ax, just like you told us the first time."

"Sure enough," Straub said, nodding his head vigorously. "I stand by my first words."

Wide-eyed and panting, Straub was led back to his cell by Loomis and Collins. Marsh walked back to the other end of the room, removing the sheet for a second time.

"Thank you for your assistance, Mr. Meadowlark,"

Marsh said, helping the man up from the table.

"Damn odd men, you all are," Meadowlark commented, removing the rope from his neck. "Damn odd white men, at that."

*****

"This is his state," Prosecutor Hatch was saying as an aside to the Jackson City manager Thomas Crary later that afternoon. They stood in the rotunda at the Michigan State Capitol, along with Governor Alexander Joseph Groesbeck. "He gets to step in whenever the hell he wants." This was in response to Crary's complaint about a local disturbance in Jackson becoming a state issue involving the governor.

"There's always somebody above us," Colonel Vandercook whispered to the men after overhearing Hatch.

The gallery was filled with newspaper men, legislators preparing for the summer adjournment, and law enforcement officials from several agencies. Vandercook must have put the fear of God into Harold Mallett and the Jackson would-be vigilantes, for they were conspicuously absent from the folding chairs in a section specifically designated for Mallett.

"No more talk of mobs and lynchings," the Governor was saying. Groesbeck was a first-term Republican governor, who would go on to serve two additional terms. He'd made a name for himself, first as a practicing lawyer in Detroit, then the Michigan Attorney General. Elected governor in 1920, Groesbeck was a bold leader from the start, tackling the problems of funding the construction of roads throughout the state, defeating attempts to abolish private schools, as well as directing prison and parole reform. Personally overseeing all pardons and paroles in the state while governor, Groesbeck was responsible for a drastic decline in the number of Michigan inmates granted parole.

"This great state of Michigan shall not erode into a state of lawlessness," he declared, taking a moment to wipe sweat from the bald top of his head. "As Colonel Vandercook has made clear to our brethren from the wonderful city of Jackson, sedition, insurrection, and general disrespect of the law will not be tolerated in any fashion. George Straub, the accused murderer of a fine, upstanding woman of Jackson, will be returned to that city, without incident, so that Prosecutor Hatch can see that justice is done in Circuit Court, not at the hands of a mob."

"Let me assure the Governor, and the citizens of Michigan," Major Marsh said, stepping forward to project his voice, "the troopers of the State Police are fully prepared for any disturbances, such as that which unfortunately occurred in Jackson Tuesday night. Furthermore, Adjutant General Bersey of the Michigan National Guard has indicated that companies of infantry are available for dispatch from Ann Arbor and Kalamazoo, with an additional battalion of guardsmen from here in Lansing, if the need arises."

The governor cleared his throat and Marsh quickly followed up his comments.

"But we are confident that that will not be necessary, as we are sure the fine citizens of this state will act in an upstanding and proper manner."

The men walked away from the crowd, and the governor took Crary aside.

"Bring in the National Guard for a pack of yokels from Jackson?" Goesbeck was incredulous. "Christ, Tom," he swore. "You get back to Jackson and impress on your people that it is their duty to keep the peace. I don't care if you have to lock up these jokers in the jail, state pen, or the armory, just keep them in line."

"Sure, Alex, sure," Crary said. He'd known

Groesbeck back at the University of Michigan Law School,

so they could speak frankly when in private.

"I heard the state boys let loose with the tear gas on

women and children, Tom. Those are voters, God damn it.

Make sure your people diffuse any situations before they

blow their top." The governor paused to again wipe his pate

and make sure that the high, straight collars of his starched

white shirt were still under his lapels. "Got time for lunch,

Tom? We'd love to have you and the missus up to the

cottage on Mackinac this summer."

"That would be swell, Alex," Crary said, pleased that

the tongue lashing was mild, not like what he was going to

give Chief Bean when he got back to Jackson.

CHAPTER TWELVE

Tuesday, June 20, 1922

The weekend passed without incident, minor nor major, as cooler heads were prevailing and the initial bloodlust for George Straub's neck at the end of a rope subsided. Harold Mallett, encouraged by Reverend Griffith and Dr. Hendricks, caught the Sunday evening Michigan Central Railroad train westward. In three days he would be back in Ontario, Oregon, with the rest of the Mallett clan, laying to rest their beloved sister and daughter, Alice. His absence from Jackson also did a lot to promote a calm citizenry.

Still in custody, their exact status in an ambiguous limbo, were Clark Meadowlark and Charlie Jackson. Both were unofficially cleared of the Alice Mallett murder, but the authorities did not wish to make any such announcement. Meadowlark would probably be given the third degree one more time before being released. Charlie Jackson was to be charged for indecency for his invasion of the women's restroom at the park outside Warren, as well as another indecency charge for a like offense he was alleged to have committed in the City of Jackson when the John Robinson Circus was in town the previous week.

For the time being they were being held, if for no other reason than their unsavory character. If that was the offense, Inspector Treece voiced to his de facto partner, Juan Piper, the county jail would be overflowing with ne're-do-wells. Several others who had been arrested during the round up of vagrants were serving ten and twenty day sentences at the Jackson County Jail. Upon completion of those sentences, they would be released once again upon the community, like the revolving door at the Central State Bank on Liberty Square or the Meade-White store in the

Ostego Hotel Building.

Tuesday morning, the action to be found in the bedroom community of Jackson, Michigan, was at the corner of South Jackson and Wesley Street, in the court of Judge Benjamin Williams for the 4th Judicial Circuit of Michigan.

Prosecuting Attorney M. Grove Hatch stood at counsel table, looking briefly at his pocket watch as all rose for the entrance of the judge. His first assistant, Arthur M. Wiggins, stood beside him, having just come from Police Court.

"All rise," a uniformed bailiff called out above the din of a bell being rung at a nearby firehouse just down the block, signaling nine o'clock. "The honorable court for the Fourth Judicial Circuit, County of Jackson, State of Michigan, is now in session, Judge Benjamin Williams presiding.

"You may be seated," Judge Williams, a man somewhere between fifty and seventy-five year of age, it was difficult to tell, said, sitting down on his large leather chair behind the bench on its raised platform. He had run for the bench and lost in 1911, and then been appointed in 1917, and then elected unopposed the following year. He would serve on the 4th Circuit for twenty more years from this day when he addressed this packed courtroom. Looking through his spectacles, the judge consulted the filings for the case before him.

At the defendant's table, George Straub remained standing beside his court-appointed attorney, perhaps the currently most-loathed individual in the county save for Straub himself. While chosen the previous week after Straub's third confession, the appointment of counsel was kept quiet until this morning so that the attorney would be free of public scorn for a few hours at least. Straub had been transported by representatives of the Michigan State Police just that morning from Lansing back to Jackson, a caravan of no less than ten vehicles packed with officers who now ringed the courtroom.

Straub was first rushed into private chambers in Police Court where Straub was served with the complaint and formally arraigned by Judge Simpson, at which time Straub met his attorney and waived a preliminary hearing. He was bound over to Judge Williams in Circuit Court where felonies were handled. In his second courtroom of the morning, Straub wore a county-supplied suit and tie beneath a soiled overcoat, and appeared bored with the hearing, not even so much as turning his head to take in the crowd of the concerned and the curious who had come to take in the proceedings. He occasionally ran his lame hand across the week's worth of beard on his face.

The gallery was overflowing with spectators. Even

though the time of the plea had not been made public, word took no time to travel. Youths under the age of eighteen were prohibited from the otherwise public courtroom, based on the fear that there would be descriptions of the offense of a most graphic nature. The male attendees of the proceedings varied in age, occupation, and attire, from doctors and lawyers in fine suits, to farmers and railroad hands in overalls. Women came dressed as if for Sunday services, fanning themselves vigorously in the increasing heat within the courtroom.

Law enforcement officers, from courthouse deputies and city officers, to State Police troopers, were present, almost outnumbering the civilians in the courtroom. Treece, Piper, Collins and Timmons sat on the first bench behind the prosecutor. Sprinkled throughout the attendees were officers in plainclothes, batons secreted beneath their coats in case called upon to quell any disturbances. A detachment of mounted troopers patrolled the courthouse grounds outside. If not for the incident outside the jail the other night, it would have seemed to be overkill, but the public had proven their potential. To the relief of the authorities, the citizens gathered for the proceedings were respectful of the venue and the occasion, hushed murmuring ceasing when the judge had entered.

"We are here for the case of State of Michigan versus one George Straub, also known as George Moore," Benjamin Williams recited, "on the charge of murder. This is an information, I presume, Mr. Hatch."

"That is correct, your honor," Hatch answered. As discussions had been held with Straub's appointed counsel over the weekend, a resolution was reached which alleviated the need to present the matter to a grand jury for consideration of indictment.

"And the defendant has waived hearing?"

"Yes, judge," Wiggins answered this time, "a short time ago before Judge Simpson."

"Very good, gentlemen," Williams said. "Mr. Wisner," he addressed Straub's appointed counsel. "I understand that we have a resolution to this matter?"

"That's correct, your honor," Wisner said, eliciting some gruff and disapproving comments from the gallery.

"I shall clear this courtroom, ladies and gentlemen," Williams said, glowering at the audience, "if any further outbursts occur. This is a court of law, not the steps outside the jail. Anyone who persists will be walking up those same steps on their way to thirty days as a guest of the county on contempt charges. Please continue, Mr. Wisner."

"Yes, your honor," he said, keeping a noticeable distance between himself and Straub. Straub looked from the judge to his lawyer, following the proceedings back and forth like a shuttlecock during a game of badminton. "Mr.

Straub waived his right to the presentment of this matter to a grand jury, and has acknowledged receipt of a copy of the information, waives any defects as to time, place, or manner of service, and wishes to enter a plea of guilty to the charge."

"And does he waive any right he has to a trial and the right to present witnesses and testimony in his defense?"

"Yes, your honor."

"Mr. Straub," Judge Williams said, directing his question to the defendant. "Have you had the opportunity to discuss these matters with your attorney?"

"Yes, sir."

"And is it your will and desire to waive your rights and enter a plea to the information, as your counsel has described."

"Yes, sir, it is." Straub's voice was quiet and distant, expressing melancholy but acceptance of his situation.

"Very well, then," Williams said, satisfied that Straub was entering a plea voluntarily. "You may be seated, Mr. Straub. Mr. Hatch, please read the information."

Calling upon his best skills of oration, Hatch read the allegations contained in the information, unable to resist thinking of those Jackson County residents surrounding him as prospective voters in the next election. He saved the finer details of the charge for the upcoming testimony.

"Mr. Wisner, having heard the information read in open court on this date, how does your client plead?"

"He wishes to voluntarily enter a plea of guilty to the charge contained in the information," the attorney answered curtly, not wishing to extend this hearing any longer than absolutely necessary. He did have less controversial, and better paying, clients to attend to later.

"Mr. Hatch," Judge Williams then said, "please call any witnesses you may have to establish a basis for this charge and the facts to which the defendant pleads guilty."

"Thank you, your honor," Hatch said. "The State calls Jackson County Undersheriff Vernon Kutt." Kutt entered through a doorway which led to a room for such witnesses waiting to take the stand, dressed in his full uniform, but for his service revolver which was missing from the holster strapped to his Sam Browne belt. Despite the fact that there were enough weapons in the courtroom to renew aggressions with the Germans, protocol dictated that witnesses surrender their sidearms when taking the stand.

Hatch led Kutt through a description of the investigation in general, and Straub's statements in particular which were pieced together from the defendant's multiple confessions. As the defendant was entering a guilty plea, and this was not a trial, details concerning other potential suspects or mitigating factors were deemed irrelevant to Kutt's testimony and therefore not disclosed.

Kutt walked the judge and spectators alike in a linear fashion, from the initial response to the murder scene at Lansing and Jefferson, to the written confession Straub had made his mark on at the conclusion of his interview with Major Marsh in Lansing. In lieu of having Coroner Mills testify, Kutt was permitted to testify as to the cause and manner of Alice Mallett's death. However, so as to not appear to be insufficient in his duties as defendant's counsel, Wisner did raise one objection when Kutt elaborated, and lingered, on the more gory and sensational details of Mallett's injuries. Judge Williams, already disgusted with the defendant, casually overruled the objection.

"The State has no additional witnesses to call, your honor," Hatch said at the conclusion of his questioning of Kutt.

"Thank you, Undersheriff Kutt," the judge addressed the witness as he stepped down from the stand. "Upon thoughtful consideration of the statement and testimony of facts presented by the witness for the State, I hereby conclude and find sufficient grounds that George Straub is guilty of the offense of murder, with no finding of any mitigation whatsoever to reduce the charge contained in the information." There were some outbursts from the gallery at this stage, just enough to induce Judge Williams to pound his gavel several times, but not to the level at which he believed clearing the courtroom was warranted.

"The defendant shall rise," Williams said, and Wisner had to prod his disinterested client to pay attention and get to his feet.

"Mr. Hatch, does the State have any reason to object to the Court proceeding to sentencing this morning?"

"No, your honor," Hatch answered, both he and Wiggins now standing.

"Mr. Wisner?"

"No, judge."

"Mr. Straub?" Williams asked, addressing the defendant. "Do you have anything to say which would justify postponing sentencing for a future date?"

"No," was Straub's answer, now looking at the judge. All concerned seemed to have the wish that this stain on the community, which had begun a mere eleven days before, be washed away and the matter completed presently.

"The respondent pleaded guilty to an information charging murder," Judge Williams read from paper on the blotter before him. "The crime in question was a most atrocious one. The respondent evidently deliberately started out to assault some woman criminally and as a part of the crime stole an ax. On Lansing Avenue, in this city which is the main thoroughfare to Lansing, is a paved, much traveled street, he accosted the matron of the Cittendon Home, which is a home for delinquent girls, as she was returning to the home about 10:30 p.m." Williams paused to turn to the next page of his notes and adjust his reading glasses.

The cynics in the audience thought the pause was more for dramatic effect, but the crowd was hanging on to every word. Why attempt to tune-in WCX 580, "The Call of the Motor City," out of Detroit for chatterplays when listeners could simply walk down to the courthouse for this type of salacious entertainment?

"He at once grappled with her, and in the struggle that ensued, he struck her twice with the ax, crushing her skull," Williams continued. There were muffled gasps from the females in attendance as if they had not heard these facts just a short time ago during Vern Kutt's testimony.

"He then dragged the woman from the sidewalk back into the shadow of some trees adjoining a vacant lot," Williams read, "where he cut the woman's dress strings with the ax, pulled down her clothes and criminally assaulted her, after which he cut her throat with the ax twice and made his escape without having been discovered."

Whether it was the increasing heat in the closed courtroom, or the details in the judge's soliloquy, some members of the fairer sex cried out with the back of their hands to their foreheads, momentarily fainting. It was high drama in Jackson.

"Hot damn," the unnamed reporter from *The Citizen Patriot* said quietly from the side of Sean Timmons as he feverishly scribbled in his notepad. "This'll make for great reading. Gonna get me one of Mr. Pulitzer's prizes."

"Good luck, friend," Timmons whispered back, plucking an unlit Gitanes from its perch behind the reporter's right ear. With his attention so rapt in getting his account of the judge's statement down on paper, Timmons figured that he could have replaced the cigarette with a snake and the reporter wouldn't have noticed.

"Respondent's previous criminal history," Judge

Williams went on reading, "so far as known to the Court is

as follows. He was sentenced from Osceola County in 1902,

to Michigan State Prison at Jackson for statutory rape on a

thirteen-year-old girl, being released in 1907. I understand

that respondent has also been confined several times for

being drunk. Respondent is in the neighborhood of forty-

three years old, never married, and has been a day laborer

formerly working in the lumber camps and is apparently

very familiar with an ax."

Williams concluded the statement of his findings and

looked up from his notes.

"Mr. George Straub," he said, "having been afforded

all rights due to you, no matter how heinous your conduct,

and having been afforded the opportunity to make a

statement in your defense, I now impose sentence. It shall

be ordered that you shall be placed in the care and custody

of the State of Michigan Department of Corrections, and transported forthwith to the Marquette Branch Prison to serve a sentence of life imprisonment at hard labor in solitary confinement."

The prison in Marquette had been built on the southwesterly shores of Lake Superior in 1889. Its remote location in the Upper Peninsula made it ideal for "lifers," as Straub would now be referred. What color had been present beneath his scraggly beard drained upon hearing the location he was to serve his incarceration. It was the singular moment of the morning in which Straub's attention was directly on the proceedings and his fate.

"A final word, Mr. Straub, before you are taken to your final mortal residence," Judge Benjamin Williams added as uniformed deputies approached the defendant with clanging shackles. Subscribers to *The Citizen Patriot*, reading the Gitanes-smoking reporter's byline later that day, would agree with the judge's final thoughts.

"Words are inadequate to characterize the crime to which you have pleaded guilty, and even if words were adequate, I would say would have no effect."

Straub was escorted under heavy guard from the courtroom, and out the front entrance of the courthouse, a phalanx of uniformed law enforcement officers clearing the way to the awaiting vehicle which had brought him from Lansing just a few hours previously. The crowd watch and commented among themselves, some going so far as to shout epithets at the convicted murdered, but that was the extent of reaction.

Several of the investigators followed the procession out of the courthouse and took in their last views of George Straub. Vern Kutt, who had taken an immediate and intense dislike of the defendant, not that Straub had any redeeming qualitites anyway, stared daggers. Treece, Timmons, and

Piper looked on with varying degrees of disinterest. There would be more investigations, more dead women and worse. This matter had reached a conclusion as far as they were concerned, and in their minds it served no useful purpose to obsess on that which was over.

"Must be messing his trousers," Kutt said to no one in particular.

"Why's that, besides the obvious?" Timmons asked.

"I heard that when they were hammering out this plea, Straub was begging not to be sent to Marquette. That lawyer of his even tried to get the Sheriff to recommend Straub be committed to the state pen here in Jackson," Kutt said. "Maybe he was thinking he could get his old cot back from his previous stretch."

"How long you figure before he gets to Marquette?" Piper now asked.

"At least a couple days," Treece answered, since

members from his post were to handle the transportation of the prisoner. "We got word that some damn fool auto workers were going to bushwack the caravan on the way North."

"So how they gonna get him there?" Piper asked.

"Train to Grand Rapids, then to Petoskey in Emmett County," Treece explained. "He'll probably spend tonight at that jail before catching the ferry to the U.P. Once at Marquette, he'll do the usual thirty-days in solitary before being put on a work detail. I think they quarry stone up there for the most part. Yup, he'll be breaking rocks for the rest of his life." Treece set his Stetson atop his head, and walked down the granite courthouse steps, his boots clopping like horse hooves on cobblestone.

"Where you off to, Art?" Piper asked after him.

"Got to have a talk with an Indian who wants to cause serious bodily injury or death to various Circuit Court judges," Treece turned and answered. "Then I figure I'm going to enjoy a glass of rye on my porch, watch my dogs." He gave a lazy salute before walking away.

"Sounds like a damn fine way to spend a day," Piper called after him, smiling to himself.

"Hey, Juan," Sean Timmons said from his side, "got any smokes on you?"

EPILOGUE

On June 21, 1922, near 3:30 in the afternoon, new inmate George Straub entered the Michigan Department of Corrections facility in Marquette. Having been sentenced the previous day to life in prison for the offense of Murder, he was christened Inmate Number 3336.

Just over one year later, George Straub's younger brother, William Claude Straub, was convicted for the assault of an eight-year-old girl. He was sentenced to a prison term of eight to ten years at the Michigan State Prison in Jackson.

In September of 1937, due to failing health and a determination that the relative risk he posed as an inmate was now low, George Straub was transferred from the facility in Marquette to his prior address, the state penitentiary in Jackson. On January 29, 1944, at about the same time of night that he had murdered Alice Mallett in

June of 1922, George Straub died in the prison hospital.